LONGTIME CRUSH

Montgomery Ink Legacy

CARRIE ANN RYAN

LONGTIME CRUSH

A MONTGOMERY INK LEGACY NOVEL

By
Carrie Ann Ryan

Longtime Crush
A Montgomery Ink Legacy Novel
By: Carrie Ann Ryan
© 2022 Carrie Ann Ryan
eBook ISBN 978-1-63695-188-1
Paperback ISBN 978-1-63695-189-8

Cover Art by Sweet N Spicy Designs

Praise for Carrie Ann Ryan

"Count on Carrie Ann Ryan for emotional, sexy, character driven stories that capture your heart!" – Carly Phillips, NY Times bestselling author

"Carrie Ann Ryan's romances are my newest addiction! The emotion in her books captures me from the very beginning. The hope and healing hold me close until the end. These love stories will simply sweep you away." ~ NYT Bestselling Author Deveny Perry

"Carrie Ann Ryan writes the perfect balance of sweet and heat ensuring every story feeds the soul." - Audrey Carlan, #1 New York Times Bestselling Author

"Carrie Ann Ryan never fails to draw readers in with passion, raw sensuality, and characters that pop off the page. Any book by Carrie Ann is an absolute treat." – New York Times Bestselling Author J. Kenner

"Carrie Ann Ryan knows how to pull your heartstrings and make your pulse pound! Her wonderful Redwood Pack series will draw you in and keep you reading long into the night. I can't wait to see what comes next with the new generation, the Talons. Keep them coming, Carrie Ann!" –Lara Adrian, New York Times bestselling author of CRAVE THE NIGHT

"With snarky humor, sizzling love scenes, and brilliant, imaginative worldbuilding, The Dante's Circle series reads as if Carrie Ann Ryan peeked at my personal wish list!" – NYT Bestselling Author, Larissa Ione

"Carrie Ann Ryan writes sexy shifters in a world full of passionate happily-ever-afters." – *New York Times* Bestselling Author Vivian Arend

"Carrie Ann's books are sexy with characters you can't help but love from page one. They are heat and heart blended to perfection." *New York Times* Bestselling Author Jayne Rylon

Carrie Ann Ryan's books are wickedly funny and deliciously hot, with plenty of twists to keep you guessing. They'll keep you up all night!" USA Today Bestselling Author Cari Quinn

"Once again, Carrie Ann Ryan knocks the Dante's Circle series out of the park. The queen of hot, sexy, enthralling paranormal romance, Carrie Ann is an author not to miss!" *New York Times* bestselling Author Marie Harte

LONGTIME CRUSH

When my best friend and I fell for the same guy in middle school, I stepped back.

I'd always expected to dance at their wedding.

Not sit in the back pew of her funeral.

I left town for my own reasons, but now that I'm back, it's clear Sebastian Montgomery isn't the same man I left.

He's hard. Broken.

And a single father to an adorable little girl.

When it turns out he's my new neighbor, I can't stay away.

But I know I'm playing with fire and the heat between us burns enough to scorch.

I thought I was over my crush.

But now it might crush me.

LONGTIME CRUSH

Prologue

Sebastian

MARLEY GRIPPED MY HAND AND I HELD BACK A WINCE. She was the one going through a contraction. I shouldn't show how much her grip hurt. But my word, the strength in her body—I didn't know how she was handling it.

"Oh, that was a bad one," Marley said as I reached for the cold cloth to wipe her face. Sweat covered her body, her hair in a frizzy bun on the top of her head, her skin alternating from a blotchy flush to a pale cream. The pregnancy had gone amazingly well. Other than the stress of everything, she did great. And here we were, in labor, about to become parents. I still couldn't quite believe it, but I wouldn't change a thing. Because I loved Marley with everything that I had.

"You are doing great," I whispered, before kissing her brow. She was icy cold, even though her skin was flushed, and I frowned.

"You feeling okay?"

She gave me a look. "I'm about to push a cantaloupe from between my legs. I'm a little nervous, but I'm okay."

She sort of slurred the words, and I straightened.

I looked over at the nurse, who narrowed her gaze at Marley before she started saying things I couldn't understand.

"Marley? Marley. Sweetheart? What's wrong?"

Marley reached out for me, but she couldn't lift her hand, then her eyes rolled back in her head, and all the machines around her started beeping.

My stomach fell and I swallowed hard, my whole body shaking.

"Sir, you're going to have to leave the room."

"What's going on?"

I couldn't focus, couldn't do anything, but people were shoving me out of the room, and words like "cardiac arrest" and "coding" filtered through the haze of my brain.

It didn't make any sense.

Marley was having a baby. She was in labor and doing wonderful. What the hell was going on?

"Wait, what's going on? Somebody tell me what's going on."

"Sir, go into the waiting room with your family. We'll come give you an update soon."

I tried to move past the small woman, but then a large nurse came forward, his muscles practically bulging through his scrubs.

"Mr. Montgomery, you're going to need to come with me."

I could still hear the sounds of the monitors blaring and people moving around.

"I need to know what's happening. That's my girlfriend in there. She's having my baby. Our baby. What's wrong with Marley?"

"Sir. Please come with me."

I didn't realize I was screaming, trying to push through, until I was through the double doors and they were calling security.

And then my dad was there. I held back the bile crawling up my throat and I looked at my father, unable to form words.

"What's going on?" Alex Montgomery asked, looking at me, then over at the nurse.

"You're going to need to tell your son to calm down, before we can let you know what's going on."

"I need to see Marley!" I called out, and then my mom was holding me, and my twin sister Aria took my hand.

The younger twins, Gus and Dara, clung to me as well. Security left us and I just stood there.

"What's going on?" my mother asked, and I looked into the eyes of Tabby Montgomery and wanted my mom to hold me and never let go.

"I don't know. Everything started beeping, and she got dizzy, and then they pushed me out. I don't know what's going on."

"I'm going to figure out what it is," Marley's dad said, rage on his face. He stormed towards the front desk as I just tried not to throw up.

"I have power of attorney. We're not married yet. We made sure I had power of attorney. I'm her contact. Her next of kin. The baby's next of kin. Right? Is that how it works?"

My family knew all of this, but I couldn't stop rambling.

My dad gave me a look. "Okay. Sit down, we're going to get you some water, and we're going to wait. We're just going to wait and see what they have to say."

He shared a look with my mom, one I couldn't read, one that made me want to throw up. Because the look of concern and worry sliding through his gaze, even though he tried to hide it, told me that this was bad.

So fucking bad.

Marley's father stomped away from the front desk and went straight to his wife. Marley's mom looked at me with broken eyes before she sat down and closed her eyes, her hands clasped in front of her.

My cousins and aunts and uncles and grandparents all wanted to be here to welcome my child into the world. To be here for Marley and me, but the waiting room was small, and only one person was allowed in the room at a time.

It had been a fight for me to be in there versus Marley's mother.

But Marley wanted me there, and we had the paperwork to prove it.

Everything about this pregnancy had been a fight.

But not Marley. She had been perfect.

"I need her to be okay, Dad."

My dad gripped the back of my neck and pressed his forehead to mine.

"You can do this. We're here. Right here."

He didn't tell me she would be okay.

Because my dad didn't lie to me. He had his own reasons for never lying, not to even blunt the truth a bit to calm somebody.

I needed my dad to lie to me right then.

It felt like an hour, four, I didn't know, but there were no updates. I just sat there, refusing to sit, as my family took turns standing with me, telling me that they were there for me. We Montgomerys stuck together.

I didn't realize that tears were sliding down my cheeks until later.

Finally, the door opened, and I looked up at Marley's doctor, the man who had been with us when we realized we were going to be teenage parents. Adults in the eyes of the law and in our own, but not according to some of the world.

I saw the grayness on his face and I didn't want him to speak. I wanted him to walk back in there and never tell us.

Silence engulfed the room, a single pin dropping would create a cacophony of sound, changing my world forever.

"Mr. Montgomery."

"What about my daughter?" Marley's dad snapped, and the doctor looked at him, then back at me, because he knew all of the issues with Marley's parents. And knew that while I had power of attorney, they were still Marley's parents. This should have been a time of celebration and stress and happiness.

But I didn't want the doctor to speak. I couldn't.

"Mr. Montgomery. Marley went into cardiac arrest. I'm so sorry, but she's dead."

He continued to say something about a placental abruption, about the taxing on her heart that they hadn't realized in time. Most likely a genetic defect that we would talk about later.

Marley was eighteen, almost nineteen.

How did an eighteen-year-old have a heart attack?

Later I would remember the screaming. That Marley's mother fell down and nurses ran to her.

Later I would remember Marley's father screaming in my face, shoving me, and my brother and father pushing the man back, telling him to shut it down.

I would remember my mother and twin sister holding me as my baby sister began to pace, texting the family group chat, so they all knew what was going on.

In the moment, I didn't know anything other than Marley was gone, but that wasn't the end of it.

I moved a step towards the doctor, ignoring the racket behind me.

"The baby?" I croaked. "Did we lose the baby?"

Had I lost my family?

Everyone went silent.

Marley was gone. How the hell had that happened? But I needed to know about the baby.

"Mr. Montgomery, your daughter is fine. She's being seen to now. Come with me."

Marley's parents began shouting again, but out of the corner of my eye, I saw my own parents holding them back. I didn't know what would happen or what we needed to do.

I didn't know what I was supposed to do.

My daughter.

We hadn't known the sex of the baby, had wanted it to be a surprise.

We had wanted today of all days to be joyous.

Not this surprise. Never this surprise.

I kept moving as I saw Leif, Nick, and Lake run into the waiting room behind me, out of breath, their eyes wide. Everyone started speaking at once, but I followed the doctor, leaving them all behind.

I didn't remember what happened next, didn't remember the route through the hallway, beyond seeing a few glances from nurses and that pitying look that made me want to vomit.

I couldn't hear anything, couldn't taste, couldn't do anything.

All I remembered was suddenly I was in a gown, wearing gloves, hands open, arms outstretched, waiting.

The nurse came forward, a small bundle in a cream blanket in her arms, a tiny little pink hat on the baby's head.

"Mr. Montgomery, here's your daughter." She whispered a few other things about passing all her tests and that the baby was healthy. About her weight and her length and the time of birth. I knew there would be paperwork later, a birth certificate to sign. All the little things that Marley and I had researched.

But what was I supposed to do now?

The nurse slid the baby into my arms, and my knees went weak. They gently settled me into a chair. I might have said thank you.

I looked down at my daughter, *our* daughter, and

tried to contemplate what life would be, what this moment meant.

Broken didn't begin to describe it. I was just shattered remains of who I should have been.

Our plans had been destroyed. Our path and promises to each other had been shattered.

Marley was gone. Dead. What did that word even mean?

I was nineteen years old. I wasn't supposed to be here alone.

Then I looked down at the scrunched-up little face in my hands, at the tiny little fingers that didn't even seem real.

And I knew, I knew that I didn't have time to be selfish. Didn't have time to wonder why.

I didn't have time.

"Hi, Nora," I whispered, my voice breaking. "I'm your daddy. I'll be here. We've got this."

I broke down, holding my daughter, the tears flowing, and knew the world had changed.

My world had changed.

Forever.

Chapter 1

Sebastian

Music blared over the speakers, but not loud enough to be distracting. In fact, it was just fine for me. I had an appointment in twenty minutes, so I wanted to focus on that rather than the headache from lack of sleep.

I knew why I wasn't sleeping, or at least that's what I told myself.

"Sebastian, did you get the coffee?" Leif asked from beside me. I shook my head.

"Nope. The line was around the building for drive-through, and the inside wasn't open, so I couldn't get anything."

My cousin and co-owner of Montgomery Ink Legacy pinched the bridge of his nose. "Seriously? How hard is it to get coffee in this town? We are right outside of fucking Denver, Colorado. There should be a coffee joint on every block."

"There is, downtown. We have Starbucks. Or more Starbucks. Your choice," Nick, my friend and other co-owner, put in, rolling his eyes.

"I'm sorry, we have the machine in the back. I can make us the fake espressos and even use your oat milk." I shrugged as I said it, but Leif just shook his head.

"No, I can make my own coffee. You were coming in, so I thought you could pick some up. I hate that our normal places closed down."

"When does the new place open?" Nick asked, frowning over his notebook.

"I was talking with Dad about it, and he said it should be within the next month. They already have the barista and baker in. They're just finalizing a few things."

I held back a snarl, knowing it wasn't their fault that things were running behind.

"They should have been the first tenants. I can't believe we let those other people move in."

I went to the back to make my cousin coffee though he hadn't asked. Leif had his hands full with a client—a full back piece that would take at least three sittings. I didn't mind helping out, especially when I needed to get my brain in the mood.

"What happened with the other place?" Leif's client, Dallas, asked, from where he was lying face down on the table.

"When we moved into this building after the fire at the old location, we knew we would be able to purchase it outright," Leif began.

I shuddered, remembering that fire. While the building itself had only been damaged and not destroyed, we had already outgrown the original Montgomery Ink Legacy location.

The flagship Montgomery Ink is a tattoo shop owned by some of my family. My aunt and uncle, as well as their friends, built it from the ground up in downtown Denver, and it was still running strong. Uncle Austin, Leif's father, would never retire if he could help it.

Eventually, other family members built another shop down in Colorado Springs. When Leif, Nick, our cousin Lake, and I had found the means, we opened our own place. We'd felt honored to use the name, which was a little daunting, but we made it. We passed the first year with flying colors and made some damn good money, but when it had nearly burned down, we hadn't wanted to stay. We rebuilt the place and had been there for another year, but then we found this other building that we could buy. It was the family's. We no longer had a landlord. We were our *own* landlords. And it had multiple storefronts where we could bring in more businesses.

There was a bike shop at the end, our shop, and some of my cousins even had their security business offices on the other end. But next to us was the café.

Or at least it had been.

Dallas frowned. "What was the name of the café before?"

My cousin grumbled. "A place called Coffee and Nuts or something?"

I held back a snort. "Nut Roasted," I corrected.

"A ridiculous name, but the two guys had the money, the means, and the talent according to everything we had heard."

"It was all a fucking lie," Nick grumbled.

"They had no idea how to run the business, their coffee ended up being shit, and they didn't have ethical work practices," I answered. "All in all, they fucked up, and we had to evict them. They didn't pay us, their company was going under, and they spent so much time smoking weed inside that they weren't actually roasting anything but themselves."

Dallas winced. "Ouch. That sounds horrible. I never went in there, and I'm not sad about that now. You have someone else moving in?"

"Yep. And this time, we're going about it a little differently," I answered.

"One of the big draws of the original Montgomery

Ink is the café next door. There is an actual door connecting the two, making it easy to go get coffee or a snack between appointments."

"I know that place. I love it. They have the best sandwiches. And the owner seems to know exactly what I want all the time."

I snapped my finger and pointed. "Exactly. Well, Hailey is the owner, and she actually married one of the tattoo artists there."

"That was handy."

I laughed and handed over Leif's coffee before sitting back with my notebook.

"Well, Hailey always wanted to franchise, but the timing never worked out. Between kids and just life, it hadn't happened."

"Is she opening, what is it called, Taboo 2?" Dallas asked.

I shook my head. "Not exactly. She's going into a partnership with the people who are going to be running the café next door. I don't know the name of the place, though."

"Latte on the Rocks," Leif answered. "It sort of plays on the whole Rocky Mountain thing, and the fact that we are an iced coffee generation. They're going to have some damn good baked goods, though. I've tried a few samples from the baker. She's a pastry chef. Went to school for it and everything. Though I haven't met her, since she's always doing a hundred things. The barista, Greer, brings everything over."

"That sounds too fancy," I grumbled. "I just want a muffin in the morning."

"I'd say something to that, but I don't know you well enough to make a sex joke," Dallas added, and I rolled my eyes.

I noticed that my cousin and friends didn't make a joke. They weren't very good at joking about sex or relationships when it came to me. I didn't blame them, but it had been five years. Five years since my world had completely changed, crashed to the ground, and I'd had to force myself up through blood and tears because I hadn't had another choice.

They should be free to make sex jokes, especially because that's just what we did. They did it with everyone else, but they were careful about me.

Everybody was so fucking careful around me.

I pushed those thoughts from my mind and rolled my shoulders back.

"They're opening soon, though, right?" I asked again.

Nick rolled his eyes. "I said as much. They know what they're doing, Hailey vouches for them, and since she's going into business with them, I trust them."

"All I know is that I want coffee that isn't burnt and is nearby. It's all I ask for in life," I said.

"You should ask for more. But yes, coffee's good,"

Dallas said, as my client walked in. We went back to work, our break done.

My client was a man in his fifties, retired military, and wanted to finish his sleeve. We had already gone through a few sketches and the outline was done. Now I got to add the color and some shading, and I liked how it was coming together. We were adding the names of friends he lost within the shading so it was just for him, while still honoring those no longer here.

I swallowed hard as I thought about it, because I honored my loss a different way. Life was way too damn short, before you blinked, it could be gone. The person you loved was no longer there, and somehow you were supposed to move on.

I needed to get out of my head, something I had gotten better at in the past five years. I just needed to remember to do so.

It took a couple of hours, and then I was done and packing up my station.

"I need to head out. I'll work on the books for Lake later," I said. Our cousin who owned the building with us but wasn't a tattoo artist, was the brains behind the business, and we wouldn't be here without her. She was also Nick's wife.

"No problem. We have a meeting tomorrow, though. You good with that?" Leif asked, stretching after his client left. Leif was working longer hours tonight because Brooke had both kids at home.

"Yeah, that's fine. Are you eating here? I know you have another client."

"Brooke is bringing the kids by," Leif answered. "Luke doesn't have practice tonight, but since my ten-year-old usually has some form of activity after school, we're going to eat dinner out while we can. Just as a family, I guess. And Landon is learning what foods he likes when we go out to eat, so that should be fun."

I smiled, wondering how on earth here we were talking about kids. Leif was just a few years older than me, and was the eldest cousin of all twenty or so of us Montgomery cousins. We were a big family, considering my dad had seven siblings, not even counting all of *their* cousins.

And all of their cousins acted like our aunts and uncles, meaning their kids were our cousins, too. Even if, technically, family trees didn't work like that.

All in all, our family was ridiculous in size, but we were close. And considering everything that had happened to us over the past years, I was glad we were close. I relied on them more than I had ever wanted to, and I wouldn't be here without them.

My daughter wouldn't be here without them.

I liked the fact that Nora had Luke and Landon to grow up with. She wasn't alone. Although Nora was five now, and she was right in the middle of them, we were still family.

"I need to go pick up Nora. I not only have soccer

practice, but there's homework because apparently, five-year-olds need homework from kindergarten, and then tomorrow is dance."

Nick just laughed. "Y'all are amazing. I love it."

"Your time's coming."

"One day. One day," Nick said with a grin, and I just shook my head, said goodbye, and headed toward Nora's kindergarten. She was in an all-day school, which was weird to me. Preschool had only been half day, and then she had gone to the Montgomery Daycare.

When I was a kid, there were so many of us that my parents and aunts and uncles had formed a daycare just for the Montgomerys and those that worked for them. They had kept it going, and now the next generation was sliding their way through. Luke and Landon were part of it, as was my daughter. My youngest cousins, who were all past daycare age, still went there, though, to help when they could. It was a good meeting place.

Soon my cousins and siblings would end up with kids of their own, and the daycare would be bursting again. But for now, we were in a bit of a break.

At least a break for them. I didn't get such a break.

I pulled into the school and waited in line with all the other parents, grateful that I had got there at least in the middle of it rather than the end. That meant I didn't have to wait for an hour for my perfect parking spot at the school, but I also wasn't waiting in the middle of the street, as people honked behind me, because I was too late.

It was never easy, but I was figuring it out. We all had. My parents, my sister, and even my cousins helped pick up Nora sometimes when I couldn't. Sometimes clients went long, or I just had other meetings. I was blessed to have my family.

Because I didn't have Marley.

I swallowed hard, wondering once again why I kept thinking about her lately.

It had been five years since I lost the love of my life. Since Marley died and everything had changed.

I'd been nineteen.

Nineteen, and thought I knew what the fuck I was doing. I'd been in college, ready to buy into Montgomery Ink Legacy and start my career. I had gone to school for business, and taken art classes on the side to ensure that I was getting what I needed to become a better artist and business owner, and Marley had been right along with me. We'd had a plan.

We dated all through high school, and even that middle school dating where you held hands at dances and looked at each other across the cafeteria at lunch. We had always been together. She had been my everything. And one time the condom broke, and Marley hadn't been allowed to be on birth control because her parents had forbit it. I'd gritted my teeth at that but once again pushed it from my mind.

And somehow, at the end of it, I held my baby daughter in my hands and felt like I was alone.

But that wasn't the case. I had my parents. My family. And though I had sleepless nights as I raised my daughter, I always had someone to lean on.

I knew I was lucky, so damned lucky, but sometimes it sure as hell didn't feel like it.

I pulled up to the curb as Nora's teacher waved and my little girl ran to me.

She had soft brown hair, still in pigtails which were a little uneven after her day, and bright eyes.

She was so beautiful and looked like a blend of Montgomery and Marley. I couldn't believe she was mine. I got out and opened the back door of my SUV, she hopped right in, and I buckled her into her seat.

"Hey there, munchkin."

"I don't know if I like munchkin today," Nora said.

I rolled my eyes, kissed the top of her head, closed the door, and waved at her teacher.

The car behind me was revving its engine, ready to go, so I quickly put the car into gear and pulled out of the parking lot.

"You ready to go to soccer practice?" I asked as I got on the road.

"Yes. I'm ready. I think today I want to be a sweeper. I don't like being a goalie. I think Molly wants to be goalie, though."

My lips twitched as she continued to talk in a never-ending rapid-fire sentence. Her best friends, Molly and Shane, were in soccer and dance with her and were always by her side.

It reminded me of when I was younger and it had been us three amigos. Me; Marley, of course; and our friend Raven. Raven had moved away for college and had only come back to visit family. Everyone grew up. Hell, I was a single dad.

That wasn't what I'd thought my life would be. But I figured out a way to make it okay.

Molly, Shane, and Nora were a team and a fierce force, and I loved that they had that, so Nora was never alone.

She kept talking about what she wanted to draw because she wanted to be an artist like me and how she wanted to be a dancer in New York, on *the* Broadway.

My lips twitched, but I kept listening, asking questions when I could.

I knew every five-year-old out there was different. Some talked a little, some never stopped talking, and some only wanted to speak when spoken to. Some loved to read. Some weren't ready to leave their picture books yet.

Nora loved to read, but she loved when I read to her the most. My father grumbled about that because he did the voices better than I did, but in the end, Nora loved her daddy. And hell, I would take that win.

Soccer went by quickly, and I rubbed the back of my neck, ignoring the looks from a few other single parents.

It had always been like that, and it never ceased to amaze me. I was there for Nora, not for the women and men who came up to me to flirt by asking how I was doing.

I hadn't dated since Marley died. I'd had a few hookups, a few dinners, but nothing more. Between starting the new business, adding on real estate, and Nora, I didn't have time.

And it was only recently that we had moved into our home.

We were renting from my family, since the Montgomerys also had a construction business that happened to own single-family units.

So I didn't have time for things like dating or the fluttered eyelashes and ways that women plumped up their breasts near me.

As if that was going to catch my attention when my daughter was learning how to do pirouettes one minute and then kicking the hell out of a ball the next.

"Well, I think she likes being a sweeper," Coach Madison said, and I laughed.

"Apparently," I agreed, smiling wide as I watched Nora kick butt.

The other coach shook her head. "If she likes that, she can stay there. But you know five-year-olds. I'm glad they follow the ball around like a group of bumblebees sometimes."

I laughed, shook the woman's hand as we said goodbye, and then Nora and I headed home.

"Did you see Shane? He did so good. He got two goals."

"And only one was ours," I said with a laugh.

"He just wanted to say hi to Molly. Because Molly was our goaltender," she explained for the fifteenth time.

I laughed, nodded, and we got out of the car. I carried two of her four bags in. How my daughter could need so much stuff throughout the day baffled me.

She was more like her mother than she would ever know.

That familiar pain settled in, but I told myself it was okay.

Marley's photos were in the house, and we lit a candle to speak to Nora's mommy whenever we could.

It wasn't the same, it would never be the same, but we did what we could.

"Get your snack, and I'll make dinner in a bit."

"Okay!" Nora called out as she began to quickly change into her at-home clothes.

I picked up behind her, sighing, and knew that would be another thing we'd have to add to her list to work on.

Sometimes she put her clothes in the hamper. Other times they were on the floor. Of course, I had always done the same thing, and it had only been moving out on my own and having to take care of not only me but Nora that I had gotten better.

I had even gifted my mom a nice thing of laundry soap in a container when I had moved out, just as a joke to say thank you. She had smiled, wiped away tears, and tried to do my laundry at this house.

I started dinner, just a quick vegetable pasta, as my phone buzzed.

I looked down and ignored it when I saw who it was.

I didn't want to talk to Marley's parents today, not when we had a hundred things to do. If they needed something, they would email or leave a message.

I gritted my teeth, thinking about the past few years. I wasn't going to worry about that just then.

We had won, and that's all that mattered.

The doorbell rang and I frowned, wondering exactly which family member it would be now. There were dozens of them, so who knew.

"I've got it!" Nora called as she ran past.

She was wearing her at-home clothes at least and not running naked to the door. She had finally gotten out of that naked phase, which I was grateful for. Trying to catch a naked toddler on my parents' lawn in the middle of winter had been a fun event for sure.

"No, you don't. You know we don't answer the door for strangers," I called out.

"Okay, fine," she said with such a put-upon sigh. I held back a laugh.

I looked through the peephole and frowned, my heart doing a little racing thing that I didn't understand.

I opened the door as Nora started to clap with glee.

"Raven?" I asked, eyes wide.

Raven looked the same as she always had, which surprised me. It hadn't been that long since I had seen her, and hell, I had just thought about her earlier that day, but for some reason, since my life had irrevocably shifted, I thought she would've changed.

I sure as hell didn't look like I had five years ago, or even last year for that matter, with the new ink that Leif had done.

She had dark brown hair as usual, but with a hot pink streak in the front and a couple on the sides from what I could see. She had strong cheekbones, dark eyes, and wore a flannel shirt over a tank top, and jeans with holes at the knees.

She looked laid back, when I usually saw her when she was at school or for something where we had to wear our best and our blackest.

I remembered the last time I had seen her.

She had been here for the funeral. She had slid in at the back and sat in the pew alone. Her cheeks had been wet. I had gone to her and hugged her tight, but we hadn't spoken. There hadn't been time. Everybody had needed me for something, and she had always shied away from gatherings where she felt in the way.

"What are you doing here?" I asked.

"I know you!" Nora waved.

Raven blinked and looked down at Nora. "Hello, Nora. I know you too. I haven't seen you in a few years, though. You were just a baby."

"But your picture is on the fridge with mommy. And Daddy. You look pretty. I like the pink."

Raven grinned. "I like the pink too." I saw the sadness in her eyes at the mention of Marley, and I wondered if it echoed my own.

"Your mom sends me photos," she said to me.

I blinked. "What?"

"Just...you know...the family newsletter stuff. I've always been on the list. Well, anyway, it's nice to see you, Nora, and Sebastian. I saw you guys pull up, so I thought I'd say hi."

She waved at the house next door, the house that had been empty the day before.

"You moved into the rental?" I asked, frowning, wondering why the hell I hadn't known.

She looked over her shoulder. "I needed a place to move in because of the shop and everything. I moved back."

Everything hurt, and I tried to keep up, only it felt like I was missing key parts of this conversation. "What?"

"I own the shop with Greer? Latte on the Rocks? I'm starting soon, and I was waiting for all of my things to get here so I could move into the house.

Your parents and I talked about it. Did they not tell you?"

"Apparently not," I said, wondering why my voice sounded so gritty.

She looked at Nora, then at me, and I noticed the light dimmed from her eyes. She no longer looked excited to see me.

But hell, why hadn't anyone mentioned that Raven was moving in next door? To both my work and my home.

"I've been in Portland, for school, and then life, but I'm back now. For my parents and because this is home. It was time."

Unsaid was why she had left. Because I still didn't know.

"I've been staying on Greer's couch while house-hunting, and then this just worked out perfectly. So I'm here and ready to settle in, and the Montgomerys have been great. And don't worry, I just wanted to say hi, and well, yeah, I'll be busy with work and everything, and I found this." She handed over a red ball to Nora. "This was in my backyard, and I figured it was yours."

She smiled brightly, but I could tell it was false.

"Thank you. I forgot that she kicked it over there."

Nora looked up at me. "Sorry. I didn't mean to."

"It's okay, munchkin."

"Not munchkin," she grumbled, and I smiled despite myself.

"It's good to see you, Raven."

"Yeah, you too. It's nice to see you too, Nora. Anyway, goodbye now."

She fled, and I felt like an idiot. I hadn't welcomed her in, hadn't said welcome home. I'd done nothing except wonder why the hell she was there. She'd been my best friend for most of my life, right along with Marley, my twin, and my cousins.

I closed the door and Nora asked a thousand questions.

Because it wasn't the shock of seeing Raven, my friend from years ago that no longer felt like the same person. No, it wasn't that.

It was the fact that I had a hard-on for a woman I knew I shouldn't.

And why the hell it had to be her.

Chapter 2

Raven

"WHY ARE YOU SHAKING?"

I looked over at Greer and frowned. "I am not shaking. I have hands of steel. I can deal with any stress, a fallen soufflé? Perish the thought. Layer is not laminating? Never. I do not shake."

My best friend blinked at me, then pointed down at my hands. "You are indeed shaking, my darling."

I followed her gaze and winced. "Ah. Well. That is unexpected."

Greer snorted. "Our opening is in three days. We are ready to go. Latte on the Rocks is what we've been waiting for. We're renting out this space. We are in a contractual obligation with an amazing café that I'm still jealous exists and am mad that I did not know about for how long now? We've got this down. The beans are ready. The equipment's in place, and the dishware is ready to go. Our staff of two part-time students is ready to go. We haven't slept in a month. You're now moved into your house. Stop freaking out."

"I'm stressed because this is a big thing. We're going out on a limb and working for ourselves. People don't do that in their early twenties. They work for others, learn the business, and then slowly and methodically work towards something like this. It doesn't happen at our age."

Greer sighed and leaned against the counter. We had gone with a white and glitter countertop. It was perfect because we had sealed it enough that no matter what we did, it wasn't porous enough to chip or stain—and glitter made us happy.

The Montgomerys—the building owners—let us do what we wanted cosmetically. A lot of the kitchen had been done by the previous owners, so we hadn't had to install new plumbing or electric. We'd had to change all of the lighting out, so it wasn't a garish yellow that made me feel like I was in prison.

Everything was open and inviting, and we used our loan and our meager savings from our families and small inheritances, as well as Hailey's investment to make this space our own.

All of the chairs were comfortable to sit in, and we even had a fireplace. It was a two-sided fireplace that we shared with the tattoo shop on the other side. So when the fire wasn't on, and we didn't have the divider up, you could see between the two businesses.

There were little tables and booths for people to sit and eat sandwiches, my pastries, and drink Greer's coffee.

We had thought about this long and hard, and it wasn't like we were starting from scratch, not with this being an offshoot of Hailey's brand, but it was still ours.

"This isn't us jumping in feet first without looking where we're going," Greer said, for what felt like the fifteenth time. Usually, it was she who was stressing out, and I was the one calming us, but being back in my town, not Greer's, it felt like I was off-kilter.

Greer was from Portland, born and raised in Oregon, and moved to Colorado because I had wanted to come home. To see my family and to start over.

To stop running away.

Even though it felt as if maybe I should have kept running.

"I know this is also Hailey's vision, not just ours, but what if this is a huge mistake? What if we go out of business in a year? The food industry is so hard. I mean, restaurants go out of business all the time. Cafés don't make it. They have cute little names, and then people stop going after a few months because they go where they know the sizing and have the name recognition."

"Everybody is always going to know how to get a venti caramel macchiato," Greer began. "And we have those here. We will have what they know and what they want. They're going to get a good cup of coffee, or a sugar fest if that's what they want. I'm going to keep them here, just like you will. You are a brilliant pastry chef. You not only can bake a loaf of bread like nobody's business, but you can also make pastries that make people weep."

"I'm making sandwiches now. That's not what I went to school for."

"You did go to school for this. Stop stressing. And you know it has nothing to do with the fact that we're opening up a new business in three days. You know it."

I narrowed my gaze. "Stop it. It *is* this. It's our future and our dream—everything could crash down, and then there'd be nothing."

"So, how is the hot Montgomery?" Greer asked, and I narrowed my gaze.

We had been drunk one night in college, laughing with each other and telling each other secrets. I hadn't meant to say this one. I had kept it bottled up for so long that not even my best friends had known, which had been a good thing at the time because my secrets revolved around those best friends.

I was the worst sort of person, and I couldn't go back

and fix it. But now Greer knew, and we were sitting in the middle of my secrets.

"Shut up."

"Does he know you crushed on him?" Greer asked, fluttering her eyelashes.

I cursed under my breath and looked around, as if one of the Montgomerys could pop up at any moment. Considering we were in Colorado, they could. There were dozens of them, maybe more. I didn't really know. I'd even seen one in New Orleans and one in Portland. They were all scattered, but they came back to their home base. Now I was in their central collection zone. They could be anywhere at any time. I was in their building. They were next door. I could see the feet of someone who was most likely one of them as they walked past the fireplace. I needed to turn the fireplace on and block the view off. Why had I thought keeping that fireplace was a good idea?

"You are currently rubbing your temple so hard you're going to leave bruises. Are you thinking about the fireplace again?"

"The fireplace is fine. I'm sorry."

"So, he knew that you used to crush on him?" Greer asked again, completely ignoring my discomfort. We did that to try to push each other toward finding happiness though. Being best friends was sometimes challenging.

"You know what? Yes," I said truthfully. "When I was still using my Trapper Keeper and before I'd even gotten my period, he knew I had a crush on him. But you know, that didn't work out."

For a multitude of reasons, namely because my childhood best friend had also crushed on him, and the two only had eyes for each other. From juice boxes on, they had been inseparable.

And I hadn't been a third wheel because they had always wanted me with them, until I left.

I pushed those thoughts from my mind and glared at Greer.

She fanned her face. "You know, he's pretty, though. They all are."

I narrowed my gaze. "Montgomerys surround us. Don't fall for one of them. It's exhausting."

I hadn't meant to let that last part slip.

"Not all of the people that surround us are Montgomerys. Yes, Montgomery Security is Montgomerys, though I'm pretty sure that there are a few employees that aren't. They don't all look chiseled from stone, with chestnut-brown hair and blue eyes that just pull you in."

She had just described nearly every Montgomery out there.

"*Greer.*"

"And many of the tattoo artists and piercers next door are Montgomerys or married into the Montgomerys. But you know, there's one that isn't."

"Greer," I warned again.

"Wyatt isn't a Montgomery. And he's pretty."

My lips twitched. "We don't have time for pretty. And Wyatt has a girlfriend."

Wyatt owned the bike shop on the other side of us. A lot of people in Colorado liked riding bikes, and he sold them, repaired them, and rented them. It was a good deal, and since he was the end unit, he had space for all of the bike racks outside. We had a full patio because of the way our building curved, so people could eat outdoors when the weather was nice. And Denver, Colorado, had beautiful sunny days. We had a lot more sunny days here than we ever had in Portland. In fact, I had to up my skincare regimen because I had started to get a little pink on my nose, something I hadn't had to deal with when I lived here growing up.

Every single part of this building seemed to work together. When Sebastian's family bought the place, they had put thought into what would go in. They had wanted a café and coffee shop, because that's what worked with the original tattoo shop, and they wanted something similar.

The previous tenants hadn't worked out.

"Knock knock," a familiar voice said from the doorway, and I looked up to see part of my past walking in.

I pressed my lips together, feeling as if I had stepped back in time and I didn't want to be there, because Marley was gone. She wasn't coming back. I needed to stop thinking about her.

I needed to stop thinking about the little girl I had

seen with her bright eyes, who looked so much more like Marley in real life than she had in the photos Sebastian's parents had sent me.

But Sebastian and little Nora weren't there, even though I was going to be forced to work next to Sebastian day in and day out. I had done my best to avoid him. I had made sure he never saw me, because I hadn't wanted to deal with the look in his eyes. I hadn't known what it would be. He had looked so angry, and lost, and yet happy to see me all at once. And that did not make any sense to me.

I had no idea what to do with him, so I just wasn't going to think about him at all.

But it was hard to do when his family stood in front of me.

"Hello, Leif," I said as I waved at Sebastian's cousin.

"Hey there, Raven. You know, when the family said you were part of the team, it didn't click until yesterday that you were *our* Raven."

"It's me. A little older, but it's me. Greer worked with you guys more than I did until now. Sorry about that. I had to move us here." I moved forward, ducking my head, and hugged him tightly. He kissed the top of my head and I rolled my eyes, but this felt a little more familiar.

Leif was at least a decade older than all of us. He and Lake, who also owned part of the tattoo shop, were close in age, while the rest of the cousins had all lumped together about ten or fifteen years younger than them.

That meant Leif had been in my life as soon as I had met Sebastian, Aria, and Marley.

"You know, every time I see you, you're getting even more bearded. How is that possible?" I asked, playing with the end of his beard.

He rolled his eyes. "Brooke likes it. And so do the kids."

Kids. Because Leif Montgomery had two sons now. It was ridiculously amazing and confounding. How had we all grown up?

"He just wants to look like his daddy," Noah Montgomery Gallagher said from behind him.

I looked over at Sebastian's other cousin and snorted.

Noah was around my age, and beautiful.

Seriously, women wept when they saw him, went down on their knees, and begged just to be in his presence. At least, that's what I jokingly said.

He was a great guy. We hadn't always been in the same school; Denver was a big place with many school districts, so it wasn't until high school that we all ended up together, and since I was a year ahead of him, we didn't become friends until later.

"You know, I always thought Austin Montgomery was hot, so I guess that's okay," I teased.

Greer clapped her hands. "You know, I've met him, and with the little silver at his temples—very hot."

Leif shuddered. "Please stop talking about my father that way."

"You should be used to it," the other man said from the doorway as he moved past Noah.

"Have we met? I don't think we've met." He held out his hand. "I'm Ford. I work over at Montgomery Security, and I hang out with this idiot," he said, gesturing toward Noah.

"We're also roommates because, dear Lord, rent is high, even when you're renting from the Montgomerys," Noah teased.

I laughed. "Tell me about it. I just rented a house."

"The Montgomerys sure seem to be taking over the world," Greer said as she tapped her chin. "How nice to see you again, Ford." She looked over at me. "We met yesterday. When you were off dealing with paperwork."

"I hear there might be pastries?" Ford asked, rubbing his hands together.

I rolled my eyes and looked over at Leif. "You're all the same. And yes, I have some test batches. Just getting the ovens ready to go for us."

Noah cracked his fingers. "You're going to need some taste testers. We've got you."

I just shook my head and gestured them towards the front bar area where people could sit and eat.

"Well, let's practice. Greer, you want to do your spiel?"

"Welcome, ladies and gents, to the time of your life,"

Greer said in a deep and smoky voice, as the guys laughed.

"Not your night job, dear," I teased, and both Noah and Ford's gazes narrowed when Leif coughed into his hands.

"Well, good to know your sense of humor hasn't waned in the years since I've seen you," Leif teased.

I shrugged. "Hey, I had to keep up with all of you guys. I've done my best. Now, you don't get to order, you get what I've been making. Sorry."

"Everything smells wonderful, though I'm allergic to cashews, hope that helps," Ford put in.

I nodded. "No cashews on the premises today, so don't worry. I can make an actual note of that and ensure that doesn't happen."

"And I don't have cashew milk today, but I will, but it won't be an issue. We're very good about cross-contamination considering all of our own allergies."

"Okay, let's taste test."

"What are we eating?" another familiar voice said from the doorway, and I looked up to see another blast from the past.

Aria Montgomery, Sebastian's twin and one of my childhood friends.

I had been best friends with Sebastian and Marley. We had been the three amigos, and no one could ever have broken us apart. Aria had her other groups of friends because she hadn't always wanted to hang out with her twin, but we had still been friends.

It was still so hard to see her because I had left, to go to college out of state, to learn my business, and to run away from something I hadn't wanted to think about.

And instead of coming back and trying to be my own person, I surrounded myself with my past.

I really wasn't doing a good job with this.

"Aria, you're here," I said as I smiled at her.

She smiled back, gave a little wave, and slid onto the seat next to Noah. "I hear there's baking. Why are all of you guys here and not over at the business?" she asked.

Aria worked at Montgomery Security, along with Ford and Noah.

She was damned good at her job from what I knew. It would be weird to be seeing each other so often, considering our workplaces were now so close.

"I'm on a break between clients, and they just finished that meeting with the Sandersons. We're here to bother them for food," Leif clarified.

"It's not a bother. We're practicing. Plus, the whole point of this, you said, was so you had a café next door like you always wanted."

Aria smiled then. "Well, everybody from our place will probably be heading over soon, as well as the tattoo shop. Legacy's been waiting for this, and I'm just glad that we're here for it."

I did my best to look nonchalant, and I had a feeling

only Greer noticed that it wasn't working. "Everybody from next door?" I asked, my voice going slightly higher-pitched.

Leif shook his head, oblivious, thankfully. "Nick is working with a client, and so is Leo, so they'll come over when they are done. Two of my staff are on their honey-moon, so they won't be around, and Sebastian is taking Nora to an appointment with her doctor."

I froze, my hands going clammy.

"Is she okay?" I asked, images of the flight back five years ago, the quiet sobbing, the screaming hitting me hard.

Leif looked up, confused for a minute at my tone, before pity and sadness spread over his face. "She's fine. Really. Sorry, it's just her normal checkup. Nora only had a half day today, so they fitted it in when they could."

Everybody nodded, and I did my best to ignore the taste of bile on my tongue. "Sorry, I'm a little wired. I blame all the coffee."

"How dare you blame my precious coffee," Greer teased as she sat mugs in front of everybody. We had both ceramic mugs and biodegradable ones.

The fact that nobody had actually ordered and Greer had just done what she'd wanted didn't surprise me because that was Greer.

"How did you know what I wanted?" Noah asked, gaze narrow.

"You'll never know," Greer said teasingly.

"She's psychic, that's how," Aria said with a laugh. "Speaking of hanging out, which we weren't speaking of, but I'm just going to change the subject, we need to do dinner to welcome you back. What do you say?" Aria asked, and then she looked over at Greer. "And, of course, you're invited. You're one of us now."

I looked at Aria, then at Greer, and smiled. "Let's do it. I'm back. For good."

As we all talked, I did my best to tell myself that this was a good decision. That we were making strides and coming into our own.

And I wasn't making another mistake.

Chapter 3

Sebastian

"IT'S LOOKING GREAT, AND I THINK THAT WE PICKED THE perfect angle for you," I said as I helped Judy off the table.

She smiled, shy as ever, and ducked her head before we walked towards the mirror. Her shirt was tucked under her bra, careful about modesty, but still showing part of her new chest tattoo.

Tears sprang to her eyes and I held back a curse, realizing that I was slacking since I didn't already have tissues ready.

Before I could think, Leo tossed me a box, and I handed over the tissues.

Judy smiled at me and took a tissue before wiping her eyes. "Sorry I'm a mess. But after so many years of this scar and hoping it would one day just go away if I used enough lotion and vitamin E and all those other creams, I'm *proud* of it. I wanted to show that it's not just a part of me, but also something I overcame. Something I traveled through."

I looked down at the crossing vines with jagged thorns and faded red, black, and multicolored roses, and nodded tightly. Judy had chest surgery more than once, and between the ports, and the surgery itself, her scars had been numerous. She hadn't wanted to hide them completely, because like she said, they wouldn't go away, so she had wanted to make them *hers*.

And I think we'd done that.

"It looks wonderful. Seriously, thank you, Sebastian."

She reached out and squeezed my hand and I squeezed right back. "You came up with the idea, I just executed it."

Judy just shook her head, wiped away more tears. "No, I said *I sort of want to cover this scar, and I don't know what I'm doing. I think I like plants*. You did the rest. Seriously, thank you."

"That looks amazing," Leif said as he came to my side. "You did a fantastic job. Both of you. If you're interested, we can take a few photos for you. And honestly, we'd love them for Sebastian's book, and ours.

We have an entire portfolio for Montgomery Ink Legacy."

Judy swallowed hard and nodded. "Just don't put my face. I don't really like to be on camera that much."

"We don't have to take a picture at all," I said honestly. Yeah, I liked showing off my work. It got me new clients and looking back at my art was good for me. But I never wanted to make people uncomfortable.

"No, I'm proud of the work, so do what you want, but just keep me private?"

"We can do that. We have social media like we said in the release form earlier, but we won't put it on there."

"If you want to showcase your work, you can, because I want to make sure you get amazing business because you deserve it. Just no faces."

"That I can do."

I whipped out my phone and smiled softly at Nora's face on my lock screen.

Judy beamed. "Is that your little girl? She's adorable."

I looked up and nodded. "Light of my life and all that. She doesn't go on social media either, so don't worry, I get you."

"It's good to protect kids. They need it." Judy looked around the shop, smiling. "Okay where do you want me?"

"Let's go over here with the black backdrop. Lake

likes to do social media correctly, so we actually have a little photo booth thing."

Julie's eyes widened. "Wow. You guys know what you're doing."

"Lake does," Nick commented, as his client let out a deep laugh.

"And Nora helped, of course."

"She is my favorite niece," Leif said with a laugh. Since Nora was his only niece, the joke worked.

Judy frowned, looking between us. "I thought you two were cousins. Or wait, are you and Nick cousins?"

I just laughed and began to take photos. "Technically we're cousins, but it's easier just to say uncles and aunts with all of our kids. Don't worry about the family tree. We don't."

I winked, which made Judy blush. "Well, your little girl and that little girl's mom must be very blessed to be part of such a big family. You guys really get each other." She smiled, and I felt that lump in my throat, ignoring the pressing looks from Leif and Nick. Judy thankfully didn't seem to notice as we went through aftercare instructions.

Judy headed out, an appointment set for our next session. I wanted to see what it looked like once she wasn't swollen, to see if it needed any additions, plus she wanted a wrist tattoo. I loved returning customers, because that meant I was doing something right.

I began to clean up my station, hurrying a bit.

"You okay?" Leif asked slowly, as he went through his notebook. He was purposely not looking at me as he said it, and I knew that was for a reason.

"I'm fine. I'm used to it."

People didn't automatically assume that I was a single father. It made sense, and it didn't hurt as much anymore. Mostly because I didn't let it.

"If you say so."

"I say so."

"What does your day look like tomorrow?" Leif asked, heading up to the front desk.

"I have two appointments, and then I need to drop off Nora. It's *their* weekend."

I tried to sound casual, but from the way that the guys looked at me, I knew it didn't work.

"Really? I feel like you just did that."

"It's every other weekend. That's what the courts say."

I gritted my teeth, then gathered up my things. "Speaking of, I have to go pick up Nora from school. We have dance class, and then dinner. Long day."

"If you need to talk, we're here," Nick murmured, and his client gave me a look. His client had been part of Montgomery Ink Legacy since we opened and knew all about Marley. Had even come to Marley's funeral. He'd also been there during the fire when we almost lost everything. He was a good man. I knew the pity on his face was because he knew exactly where I was going this weekend.

Every other weekend Nora went to her grandparents' house—Marley's parents. In most cases that would be fine, it wouldn't be a cause to worry and no one would stress out. In my case, it was a ball full of pity and guilt and horridness.

Marley's parents had never liked me. When we were just kids running around in a wild trio of me, Marley, and Raven, her parents hadn't liked me. I had been the boy in the girl group, and they hadn't understood that. And when we had started dating, they hated the fact that it was me Marley had chosen. They hadn't liked how loud my family was, that we were tattooed and pierced and too crazy for them.

They hadn't liked the fact that my family owned businesses and were blue-collar all the way.

We took care of our own, and we might be loud and love cheese, but we worked our asses off and were always there for each other. Each of us as teens, while still in high school, held part-time jobs. We all learned responsibility and how to take care of family.

We hadn't been the right people for Marley, according to her parents.

Marley's parents were ultra-religious, so the fact that Marley and I had not only had premarital sex, but had gotten pregnant out of wedlock, had been the final straw.

They'd thrown away Marley's birth control pills, because in their mind if Marley didn't have birth control, she wouldn't have sex. And condoms, as everybody knows, weren't one hundred percent preventive. So, one had failed, and we ended up with Nora. And I would not regret having Nora in my life no matter what.

Nora's grandparents hated me. Because according to them it was because of me Marley wasn't here. And I had to face that every time I saw them.

I said my goodbyes and headed toward Nora's school to pick her up. This afternoon was only a short dance class, a meeting for the parents while the kids worked out some energy. Maybe forty-five minutes they told me, so I knew it would take an hour, and then I would have to untangle Nora from her two best friends, Molly and Shane, and then we could head home and make dinner and get ready for the last day of the week. The last day of the week that happened to be the opening day for the café next door, so I knew that our new neighbor would be busy too.

And then after school I'd have to give my daughter over to Marley's grandparents. Because that's what the courts said.

Marley died before she had ever been able to hold Nora. She'd not only had a heart attack while giving birth, something not unheard of but very rare, by the time she'd made it through, she'd ended up with an embolism that had taken her fully from us.

I hadn't been there for the birth. I'd been forced out into the waiting room. And when I was finally able to hold my daughter, I knew that I'd never hold Marley again.

Marley's parents had tried to take Nora from me right away. They hadn't thought I was fit as a father, even though I was an adult, with a full-time job and going to college, they had wanted to raise Nora their way.

Then they had taken me to court.

It cost me thousands of dollars just to prove that I was fit to be Nora's father. They had railed and rallied against me, had used their strict upbringing and their connections with their church and the local politicians to get what they wanted.

In the end they failed. The big and brash Montgomerys with all their ink and piercings and tattoo shops and construction work had won. Only I still had to give my daughter to them two weekends out of the month so they could spend time with her.

And I hated the fact that I couldn't say no. I wanted Nora to know her family, and not just mine. I just wished that Marley's parents would get it through their skulls that they didn't have to hate me in order to love her.

I pulled into the school parking lot and Nora ran right to me.

We had our routine—I got her into her seat and she

spoke the entire time, never stopping for anything other than breath.

"And then, Molly said that she was going to go as the purple princess, so I'm going to go as the pink one, and Shane said he would go as the blue prince but now he might want to be a princess just so that way we all match. We don't really know because we have to figure out the costumes but what do you think?"

My temples ached and I looked back up into the mirror so I could see her face.

"For Halloween?"

"Yes. But we might want to change this too. Because what if we don't want to go as the prince and princesses of Color Pop?"

Color Pop was a random TV show that made my ears bleed, but the kids loved it. Of course, she had wanted to be Marvel characters with them the previous week, and before that, something from the Adams Family. She'd even mentioned her favorite Disney Princess, Ariel. She'd most likely end up with two costumes. One with her friends for their party and trick or treating, the other for the Montgomery party we were having at my house Halloween night.

"Okay, Halloween is coming up, so how about next week when you're home from Grandma and Grandpa's, we'll go over everything together. Me and Molly's and Shane's parents can sit down and we'll make a group costume decision together. But once we make the decision, we have to stick with it."

Nora pressed her lips together, tapped her chin with her tiny little finger and looked deep in thought. I had to press my lips together as well, so I didn't burst out laughing. Seriously, my daughter was fricking adorable. I put my eyes back on the road and pulled into the dance studio's parking lot.

"I think that's reasonable," Nora said, and I held back a laugh.

I got out of the car just as Molly's mom got out of her SUV. Little Shane and Molly hopped right out and waved. The three hugged each other, dancing around as if they hadn't seen each other less than ten minutes ago.

I met Molly's mom's gaze and rolled my eyes.

She laughed. "They went with Color Pop?" she asked, her voice high-pitched at the end.

I shook my head and gestured for the kids to head inside.

"Apparently. I told Nora that I'd try to get us all to meet next week so we can make a decision."

"Sounds good. Molly's dad is out of town for the next two weeks, but then he comes home and will be home for the rest of the year, thank the gods," she said.

Molly's dad was a contract worker who was out of the country for long stretches of time. It sucked, but it was good money. Shane's parents both worked full-time, so we took turns with carpooling. The only reason we hadn't driven together today was since Molly and Shane lived in the same neighborhood, we took turns when we could.

The dance meeting was simple, mostly prep for the holiday pageant, something to do with snowflakes and glitter. I sighed and took notes because I would have to make Nora's costume. I might be an artist when it came to drawing, but I could not sew correctly to save my life.

Molly's mom looked at me and raised a brow. "Are you going to need help this year?"

I shook my head. "No, I think one of my cousins can help. My family is always up in my business for something, might as well use it for good."

She laughed. "Well, I may need to hire them, because I have no idea what I'm doing, and we both know Shane's parents aren't going to have the time."

I nodded tightly. We took turns, trying to help each other out. Molly's mom was an amazing baker, so she always helped with the baked goods when it came to all three kids. Shane's parents did weekend sleepovers, and any time there was a group event over the weekend for more than a few hours, they took care of it. I tended to work on weekends because it worked better for my clients, so our three families working together was like having an extra family unit.

"I'll see what my mom says. They're all really good about helping out."

"Thank you. Seriously. I cannot sew. I wish I could

just pick something out of a catalog, but that would probably be ridiculously expensive."

"I feel you."

We took our forms in, and then I piled Nora back into the car, pulling her away from her two best friends.

"You'll see them tomorrow at school. It's fine."

"But I *love* them," Nora said so dramatically, I resisted the urge to roll my eyes.

"You'll see them all next week too."

"But Molly and Shane are going to have tea this weekend. And I can't."

I sighed, hating this part. "I'm sorry, pumpkin. But your grandparents are excited to see you."

I had no idea if that was the case or not, but I would lie to protect my daughter. I didn't fucking care.

"But I don't want to go," Nora said, tears beginning to fall down her cheeks.

I felt like I'd been kicked in the gut. I hated this, and there was nothing I could do about it. I pulled over into a parking lot and turned around to look at her.

"I'm sorry, baby. But you love your grandparents. And they love you. It's your time with them. It's always good to have time with your family."

"I want to stay with other Grandma and Grandpa. I love them. Can't we live with them again?"

I shook my head. When Nora had first been born, I moved back in with my parents, instead of staying in the small apartment I had shared with a few of my cousins.

It was just easier for everybody, and I relied heavily on my parents and their big hearts for the first few years of Nora's life. Nora had shared my room, because I hadn't wanted to part with her, and eventually she ended up with her own room at my parents' house, and my parents hadn't batted an eye. They'd given up everything for me and my siblings, and then for their grandchild.

When we moved into the rental we were currently living in, Nora had hated leaving her grandparents, and so had I. But we had needed the independence, and now we were a unit.

Only, every other weekend, it felt like hell.

"You'll have fun. You always do."

She pouted, then wiped her tears. "Okay. I'll go. I guess. But it just makes me miss Mommy more." She rubbed her tummy, and I reached out and squeezed her little foot.

"I miss Mommy too. But I love you, okay? I love you so much."

She nodded and wiped her tears, before she went on about her Halloween costume, using that resilience of any five-year-old.

I swallowed hard before pulling back onto the road, grateful we weren't far from home. We needed to make dinner, go through homework, and I needed to find someone to help me sew. Because it sure as hell wasn't going to be me.

We pulled into the garage, and saw Raven struggling with a large box out of the back of her SUV.

"Can we go see Raven?" Nora asked, clapping her hands, tears long forgotten.

I sighed, wondering why I felt so weird. Raven had been our best friend, too. Nora knew her face, knew that she had been friends with Marley. This shouldn't feel weird, but it did.

"Let's go help," I said, after I got out of the car and Nora unbuckled herself, a big enough girl to do it. And didn't that just break my heart. How the hell was she growing up so fast?

We moved towards Raven, as she was still struggling, and I picked up the pace. As she stumbled, I reached around her, gripping the bottom of the box, my front pressed to her back.

She screamed, then looked over. "Oh my God. You scared the shit out of me." Then she winced, seeing Nora. "I mean crap? Is that a curse?"

"It's not a curse because adults can say it. But I can't," Nora explained. "We're here to help."

I was still pressed directly to Raven's back, and I did my best to will my cock to behave, because if I wasn't careful, she was going to feel exactly how excited I was to see her. And that was not something I wanted to think about.

"Oh, I've got this. Thank you."

"Here, seriously let me help." I lifted the box as she

wiggled out from between me and her car. That wiggling sent that very luscious ass of hers to press against me even more, and I swallowed hard, angling so she wouldn't feel me. Apparently I needed to get laid because just that slight friction nearly sent me over the edge. I was blaming the length of time, not the fact that it was Raven. Because fuck that.

"Where is this going?" I asked, as I hefted the box. It was heavy, but I worked out. Probably too many hours because of said tension, but I again pushed those thoughts from my mind.

"Oh you don't have to help. Seriously."

"Let me help. I've got it."

"Daddy's strong. He has all those muscles," Nora explained as she took Raven's hand and led her into her own house.

I just shook my head, as Raven blushed.

"Well, I'm grateful for those muscles." She sputtered, looked at me, and looked away, as I followed her into the living room.

"Right here's fine. They're more of my pots and pans from storage. You know, pastry things."

"You bake? Aunt Aria said you bake."

"I do. Do you like baked goods?"

"I love cupcakes."

"Well, are you allergic to anything?" Raven asked sweetly, as she knelt down to Nora's level.

I set the box down, shaking my head, wondering why

it felt as if Raven and Nora had known each other forever, even though this was one of the first times they were actually meeting since Nora was an infant.

"Nope. I'm good. I love cream cheese frosting though. At least that's what Daddy says."

Nora looked at me with wide eyes, pleading, and I saw the glint there.

I shook my head. "You're a menace. But yes, we both love cream cheese frosting. But please don't bake anything for us. You already see how hyper this one is without the sugar."

Raven laughed. "I always need taste testers for the café. However, I will not add sugar highs to the agenda." When Nora pouted, Raven laughed. "Hey, even I get sugar highs sometimes and then I'm scary to be around. I understand."

"You're not scary, you're beautiful." Nora reached out and played with the pink strand of Raven's hair. "I love this."

Raven's whole face changed, going a little wide-eyed and sweet.

Raven was gorgeous, but she always had been. "We're not coloring your hair pink. Your school won't let it. You know it."

"Okay. But Aunt Maya said maybe one day."

My Aunt Maya had multicolored hair a lot of the time, as did her children. But her children were my age, so that was fine.

"Maybe one day. But not right now."

"I didn't get pink hair until I was in my twenties," Raven explained.

"But that's so old," Nora said, with the innocence of a five-year-old.

Raven snorted. "Please say that around your Aunt Aria. Just so I can see the look on her face," Raven teased.

"I'm standing right here as well, and I'm not old," I said, teasing, as I held out my hand for Nora. "Let's give Raven some privacy. We have homework to do, and dinner."

"Okay. Bye, Raven. I like your hair, and your cupcakes. And I'll see you soon?" She waved, before she skipped away, talking me with her. "I'm leaving now."

"Thank you for everything. And I'll see you tomorrow for opening day."

I nodded tightly. "Good luck. And we Montgomerys will be there. We support local businesses."

"Especially your renters," she teased. I wondered why that teasing did something to me. What the hell was wrong with me?

I left, and told myself that I was just tired, I wasn't losing my mind. But I had a feeling I was once again lying to myself.

Chapter 4

Raven

"ARE YOU READY FOR THIS?" GREER ASKED, RUBBING HER hands together.

I wanted to throw up, and I didn't know if it was nerves or cramps. It was probably a mixture of both, which wasn't a great thing for a baker who had been up since three in the morning. I normally kept baker's hours, but I wasn't even sure I had truly slept the night before.

I looked over at Greer and I knew she was just as nervous as I was, but better at pretending. She looked excited, eager, and ready to dance the night away.

I also knew she was probably going to throw up later, because the nerves would get to her.

I held out my arms in answer, and she threw her arms around me and hugged me tightly.

"Let's get this done," she whispered, then kissed my cheek.

"You know, when only four people show up and they happen to be Montgomerys, at least we can say we tried."

I ducked as Greer slapped me upside the head. "No, we're not doing that. We are doing happy things. We're thinking happy things. Don't put that out into the universe. You know better than that. Okay, get back to baking, I will go open the doors."

"No, I'll go open the door with you," I said, as I straightened my apron. "We do this together."

Both of our staff members held up their thumbs. I smiled at them, as we walked to the door as a unit. We wouldn't always have a staff of four, in fact we rarely would. But it was day one, and even if nobody showed up, despite the advertising, the samples of sweet treats, and other things we had done to promote our business, we all wanted to be there on the first day. I just really hoped this wasn't all for nothing.

I looked through the glass doors finally, and nearly tripped over my feet.

It was six a.m., early for most people, and around the time we would be opening our doors every day of the week. We knew that people needed coffee on their way to work, so we would be early risers. I really hadn't expected anybody to actually be waiting outside though.

"Oh, my goodness," Greer whispered, and I saw her whisk away a quick tear.

Because, at six o'clock in the morning, on a Friday, we had a line.

We opened the doors quickly, and Greer beamed.

"Welcome to Latte on the Rocks. We are so happy to have you."

Hailey, our co-owner, investor, and patron, beamed at us. "I brought the whole family, and while I may be first in line, I'm happy to say that it's not just Montgomerys and friends here." Hailey hugged us tightly, and then we all got to work, doing a thousand things at once.

Hailey and her husband Sloane came in first and ordered, gushing over the look of the place. Considering this was her franchise, and we were just part stakeholders in it, it felt as if we were blessed by our own fairy godmother.

The next set of customers were of course Montgomerys, these from the downtown tattoo shop, before they headed back over to their section of the city.

I worked behind the counter along with Greer, making orders. Our staffers went to the tables, cleaned them up, made sure everybody was happy. I handed out banana nut muffins, pumpkin cheesecake muffins, honey oat squares, cranberry cheesecake buttons, various cinnamon rolls, brownies, and cupcakes, and never stopped moving.

I pulled out the biscotti on its second bake and set them to cool, before I mixed up another round of biscuits, as somebody ordered a full dozen. I also had sandwich bread and rolls cooling on the racks, as another person ordered a whole baguette.

I knew that it wasn't always going to be like today, that no matter what I baked, somebody wasn't going to like something, or I would make too much of one thing or not make enough of the other. And while I had worked in bakeries and cafés ever since I was first able to work, I didn't have decades of experience. I knew what I was doing, but there were going to be mistakes.

I needed to get those thoughts out of my mind, because I needed to focus.

I turned to the counter, going to refill the display case I was sure had already been emptied, and looked up to see Wyatt.

He grinned at me and gestured towards the stack of cream cheese blondie brownies in my hand. "Those look decadent."

"It's her own personal recipe," Greer teased.

I blushed and shook my head. "Anything here is my own personal recipe, but they're a common baked good."

"There's nothing common about you, Raven," Wyatt teased.

From the twinkle in his eyes, it took me a moment to realize that he was flirting with me. Wyatt, the bike store owner, and our working neighbor, a man who was slowly becoming our friend, was flirting with me.

Greer raised her brows as she went to make a peppermint white chocolate latte for the next customer.

Wyatt beamed at me, and asked me something, though I wasn't really paying attention. Because someone else walked into the building, and why did it feel as if I was losing my mind?

"Raven?"

"Huh?" I asked, pulling my gaze from Sebastian as he walked in, his gaze on me.

"May I have one of those brownies? Or are they for another order?" Wyatt asked.

I cleared my throat and gestured. "Of course. Let me wrap that up for you."

"Thank you. I'll go eat it over in my shop, and thank you guys for opening, because I already had people browsing in my shop, and that means more business for all of us. You should let me thank you one time. With dinner."

Sebastian, along with Noah, Ford, and Leif stood behind Wyatt, waiting to hear my response.

"Oh. Well. Here's your brownie. Thank you!" I spluttered, completely ignoring the fact that I was pretty sure he had just asked me out on a date.

Wyatt's face fell, before he rolled his shoulders back

and turned to our staffer at the register. "Thank you, Raven. And I think I'm going to have to try a little harder. Or just enjoy the sweetness that is this brownie."

He winked again as he walked out, nodding at the Montgomerys. "Neighbors," Wyatt said.

"Hey there, Wyatt," Noah drawled, before he glanced at Sebastian.

I did the same, and realized that Sebastian was stone still, hands fisted at his sides.

That was so weird. Why was he standing there? Maybe he didn't want to be here. That would make more sense. They'd probably forced him to come over because they wanted to support a local business, their neighbors, but he probably had a thousand things to do. He was a single dad, and Nora seemed to be constantly on the move. She had a zillion different activities, and Sebastian was always there for her. He didn't have time to come and see the opening of our café.

"It's the Montgomerys," Greer teased, as she hip-checked me. "While Raven is over here in la-la land, how about I take your order?"

I shook my head. "I need to go to the back. I think something's buzzing."

"Just your brain," Greer mumbled, as Noah leaned forward.

"The place looks great. I mean, not only does it look great aesthetically, but everything smells divine. We can smell it through the walls though, so I'm grateful that we built the door from the café to the tattoo shop. Can I just say, it was the best idea ever?"

"We blatantly stole that from your father's shop, Leif," Greer put in.

"Oh, when we first renovated this entire building as we bought it, we made sure that that was going to happen. The people before you really weren't into the idea, but you guys are. And that means we can get coffee and baked goods and sandwiches when we need it, and I just know I'm going to have to add, like, two more workouts to my week in order to survive all of this sugar."

I shook my head. "We'll make sure you eat healthy, too. I don't want to deal with Brooke when I get you on a sugar high."

"Just don't let the kids have all the sugar without me knowing, okay?" he teased.

"Don't worry. I'll be good. Maybe." It was easy to talk with Leif, because he was like a big brother, just like Ford and Noah were. Just family, reminding me of a time long past.

Sebastian though, Sebastian made me feel weird. There was nothing more to say about that.

I was nervous, warm, tingly, and wondering what the hell I was going to do.

Because that middle school crush was long gone. This was Sebastian Montgomery. He was different now.

And he wasn't and couldn't ever be mine.

"Do you have some form of sandwich?" Sebastian asked, his voice a deep growl.

Ford glanced over at Sebastian, brow raised, and I wondered why Sebastian sounded like that.

He really didn't want to be here. But this was our opening day, so I was going to be good.

I wasn't going to let my disappointment and the fact that it looked like he wanted to be anywhere else but here show.

"We do have sandwiches. They're on the board, or I can make you something."

"Wait, you're going to make him a special sandwich and not me?" Noah asked, aghast.

"I can make special Montgomery sandwiches. How's that?" I said on the fly. Leif beamed but Ford just glared.

"I'm not a Montgomery. I might play in the same sandbox, but I have my own name. And my own set of brothers."

"Oh yes, the Cage brothers," Noah said with a roll of his eyes. "You don't want to mess with them."

Intrigued, Greer leaned forward. "There are more of you? Keep talking," she teased.

I shook my head. "Get back, we have work to do. And I have sandwiches to make. Although I'm sorry, I kind of like the idea of calling it the Montgomery sandwich."

"Fine, but you're going to need to make me a Cage sandwich."

I laughed. "I can do that. Specialty named sandwiches on the way."

Sebastian didn't say anything, and I was glad for it.

Something was weird, then again it had been weird between us for a while now. Even before Marley had passed away. Because I left, and he stayed, and he had never forgiven me for abandoning Marley.

BY THE TIME THE DAY WAS OVER AND WE CLOSED UP SHOP, my feet ached, my back ached, and I was pretty sure that I was so wired on sugar, I wasn't going to be able to sleep.

Greer was ecstatic and did a backflip in the parking lot before we left. I just laughed and headed home.

It wasn't always going to be like this, there were going to be bad days, but today was a damn good day.

Greer was amazing at social media and had kicked ass making sure people knew we were there. She had even done a few live feeds from when we were working, getting people to laugh as they teased about the wait and the fact that they were dying in gastronomical bliss once they got their orders.

They loved our food, loved our coffee, and loved our place.

We just needed to make sure they kept coming back.

I pulled into my garage and noticed that Sebastian's

front lights were on, but I didn't look for too long. Instead, I closed the garage door behind me, and put those thoughts out of my mind.

He didn't want me here. That much I had figured out. I just wanted to know why.

Beyond the ideas that I already had.

I went inside, put my things away, and decided that maybe a long bath before my early wake-up call for our second day was what I needed.

I stood in front of the bathroom mirror and slid my fingers over my necklace.

It was one-half of a heart, layered with the other half that I should never have had.

Marley and I had given them to each other when we were in middle school, and I'd had to put the piece on another chain when I'd gotten older.

Marley's parents had handed it back to me, along with a few other of my things that had been in her child-hood room. They hadn't wanted anything to do with me, or their daughter's past when she died. I didn't always wear the necklace. In fact, I rarely wore it. There was no need to wear something to remind me of my former best friend when all I had to do was close my eyes and I could see her smile, and the way that she lit up the room.

But I had wanted her to be part of today. She had always loved my baking and had pushed me to pursue my dreams. Even if it meant leaving her and Sebastian behind.

I let out a breath when suddenly dizziness swept over me and I clung to the bathroom counter.

When bile rose up, I staggered to the toilet, and threw up everything I'd eaten that day, even though it hadn't been much.

Cramps assailed me, and I kept throwing up, sweat pouring off my face, before I lay on the cold tile, shaking, hating myself.

I curled into a ball, wondering why I had let myself forget.

I had been too stressed that day and hadn't taken care of myself. I had just wanted something for myself. Just once.

Because it wasn't always like this. Sometimes I actually didn't hate myself. I didn't hate my body.

But today my body hated me.

And it reminded me once again, that life was never as it seemed.

And I didn't always get what I wanted.

Chapter 5

Sebastian

I WIPED THE SWEAT OFF MY BROW, ANNOYED THAT IT WAS so muggy in my small mudroom, when it had been cold a couple of days prior. That was fall in Colorado, you never knew what the weather was going to be. I paused in my thinking, bending down to pick up my paintbrush. Honestly, that was *every* season in Colorado.

Sweat continued to pour as I worked on the trim, grateful I was nearly done with this part. I preferred rolling to trim, but someone had to get it done. Of course, my family who did construction were a thousand times faster and better than I was. They weren't offering to help, though. I set the paintbrush back down, and then stripped off my shirt, wiping the sweat from my face completely.

I hated weekends like this. I should be working, I should be going over portfolios, drawings, and even doing actual tattoos. I had clients that I could meet with this weekend, but the way things had worked out, today it had been better for me to stay at home for the afternoon and get household things done that I couldn't really do well when I had Nora.

I held back a sigh.

Because Nora wasn't here. I had dropped her off at her grandparents' that morning, had done my best not to snarl at the way Marley's parents glared at me, and then watched my little girl roll her shoulders forward, and look defeated as she went to the people who I knew loved her but didn't understand her.

They had been the same way with Marley. They'd loved their daughter. Loved her to the point that they were breaking what they had with Nora.

I missed my kid.

I had never once thought that I would be a father this young. In fact, I thought I wouldn't be a parent until I was in my thirties or something, much like a lot of my uncles. But no, I'd been a teenage dad, and I had only made it work because of my family.

I hated the fact that my kid wasn't here.

So here I was, repainting my mudroom in the back of

my house because we had let it go a little bit. The place was owned by my family, the entire Montgomery realty section of our conglomerate. I snorted at that, considering our conglomerate was just a small grouping of companies that we happened to own. We weren't ruling the world, much to the surprise of everyone around who knew us.

And so, while I didn't need to do my own mainte-nance, I knew how. My cousins in the construction arm of the family were better at it, but I could paint a mudroom.

Eventually I would have to redo the laundry room that was connected to this room, but I wasn't in the mood to move all the appliances around, so I would do that later. Or maybe I would do it tonight when I couldn't sleep because I missed my kid, and it wasn't like I had a nightlife. My cousins and brother wanted me to go out, even my twin was trying to force me out of the house, but I just didn't want to today. I wanted to wallow in my own guilt and shame.

"Knock knock."

I turned, paint roller in hand, to see Raven walking up to the house. She met my gaze, then her gaze went a little lower, and she blushed and tripped. I cursed and moved towards her, the door already open so I wouldn't touch anything with the paint roller.

"Sorry, there was a tree root or a hole. Or just my own feet. I trip a lot."

My lips threatened to twitch into a smile. "I hope you don't do that when you are around ovens."

She winced, looked down at her arms. "Well, I do have a few burns from pans, but that's just the life of a baker. I'm pretty sure I permanently have flour in my hair."

I looked up, shook my head. "Don't see any."

"I did just shower, so thanks."

Images of Raven taking a shower filled my brain and I quickly pushed those from my mind. What was wrong with me? I did not think about Raven this way.

"Well." She looked me up and down, and I willed my cock not to react. Because it was a slow perusal, and damn it, it was a perusal. "You used to be scrawny."

I snorted, grateful for the humor. She wasn't hitting on me, not like some women did, she was just being her old Raven self. And that's what I needed. Not whatever this attraction between us was that sometimes seemed to rise up.

"I lift things," I said deadpan. "It's fun."

She raised a single brow, and I was kind of jealous she could do that. "And all the ink? That's new."

I did have more ink than a lot of my cousins. I worked in a tattoo shop, and my family was really damn good at it. I also happened to like the art, so I just shrugged, knowing one day I might run out of space. But I didn't think so. I had a few pieces on my chest, down my arms and back, but I still had a lot of space.

"I'm a tattoo artist."

"And so that means you like tattoos?"

"I would hope so. I like ink, piercings, too."

She looked up at my eyebrow ring, and then lower for an instant, before she blushed and turned away.

I wasn't going to tell her that yes, my dick was pierced, because I didn't really know how to bring that up in a conversation. As it was, my cock was trying to get up all on its own.

"I still need one."

"A piercing?" I asked, willing myself not to look down at her breasts, or at her clit. I did not need those images for my mind, but they were there. And all I wanted to do was see if she was pierced. Or pierce her myself, or lick at those piercings, just to see if they could make her come.

What the hell was wrong with me?

This was Raven. I didn't have an attraction to Raven. She was my friend from childhood. Nothing more. Now she was my fucking neighbor.

"Uh…I mean, a tattoo?" I blurted.

Her eyes widened. "I have my ears pierced, that's it. And no tattoos. Virgin skin and all that." She blushed again, harder. She was so pretty in pink. "I mean, my skin doesn't have ink on it. I don't need to mention virgins."

I held back a groan, what the hell was wrong with us?

"Well, that sounds like a challenge." I paused, as we both burst out laughing. "I meant a tattoo if you wanted it. Not anything else. I'm going to change the subject now."

She grinned. "I just finished my walk after a long day at the café, and saw the door was open." She looked around. "Where's Nora? I assumed she'd be running out here to ask a thousand questions."

Immediately my mood dimmed, and I shrugged. "She's with her grandparents for the weekend."

Raven winced. "Ouch. I'm sorry."

Confused, I frowned. "What do you mean by that?"

"I know her grandparents, Seb. I know about the court case. And I know that this weekend probably sucks, hence why you're shirtless and painting and even talking to me out here."

I gritted my teeth, hating the fact that she knew all of that. I tried not to let it show because I didn't want Raven to feel like anything was wrong.

"It's fine."

"It's not, and I'm sorry."

I sighed, knowing it was the truth. "It's not fine." I set down the paint roller, rolling my shoulders back. "Why did you leave?"

"What do you mean? I had to work this morning, and Greer's closing the shop today. I close tomorrow."

I shook my head. "No, Raven. You *left*."

I hadn't meant to say any of that, to bring it up. But

it had been on my mind since we were eighteen, and I'd never asked. First, because I'd been so into Marley that I'd had my head up my ass and hadn't wanted to ask the big questions, then because it had gotten too difficult.

She pressed her lips together, then let out a breath. "Yes. I left for college to learn how to run a business. You and Marley stayed." She flinched. "I'm sorry I keep saying her name."

I shook my head, that ache at hearing Marley's name a familiar one. It had dulled a bit, wasn't so sharp, but it was still an ache. I didn't think it would ever go away, not that I wanted it to. I wanted to remember Marley. It wasn't fair not to. "If I don't say her name, it hurts Nora. So I do."

Raven studied my face for so long I wasn't sure what she was going to say, or if it was better for her to just leave.

"And it hurts you."

"I get over it." I turned then, needing a moment to collect myself, as I went back to painting. She could go or she could stay, I couldn't care less. Okay, that was a lie, but I didn't want to care. I didn't know what was happening, didn't like these feelings, and I didn't like change. I just wanted things to stay the damn same. Why couldn't things just do that?

Raven moved closer, and I could feel the heat of her.

"You don't get over it, Seb. And that's fine."

Why did she keep calling me Seb? As if we had a

shared history. We did, but I didn't want to acknowledge it. I just wanted her to go away. But I wanted her to stay.

"Why did you come back?" I asked, far more harshly than I intended.

Raven picked up a paintbrush, working on the corners even though I hadn't asked her to. I didn't want her to. This was my project. For my house with my daughter. Why was Raven here?

She shouldn't be here.

Marley should be here, but she was gone, and I was over that. As much as you could be over someone dying. I mourned, I grieved, but it wasn't all-encompassing anymore.

But every time that my kid went to her grandparents, it hit me, and now Raven was here and that just made it all worse.

"I wanted a new life, that's why I left before." There was something in her tone, something I should ask about, but I didn't. "But now I realize that my life was here all along. My family's here. My friends. So I'm starting over, a new business, a new part of me. I didn't realize that you'd be so close for all parts of it."

I swallowed hard and looked down at her, doing my best not to think about her. Hard to do when all I could do was smell her, even over the scent of paint. She was so damn beautiful, had always been. I had never thought about her that way before. It would've been unfair to Marley, a betrayal. But I had known that Raven was beautiful and kind. We'd been friends for a reason, because we meshed.

And now, everything ached.

I didn't know what it meant.

She was so damn close to me, her body sweat-slick from her walk, just like mine was from the heat of this room. We were close enough that all I had to do was lean down ever so slightly, and brush my lips against hers. But I wouldn't.

Because that would be the most insane thing I could have ever done.

"Your life is here. It never made sense for you to leave."

Once again she was quiet for so long, I didn't know what I had said wrong.

"It made sense at the time."

"Sebastian, where are you?" a familiar voice echoed from the front of the house, and I whirled, Raven doing the same so we crashed into each other. I dropped the roller and gripped her arm, grateful that we both didn't tumble into the paint pan.

And that's when my parents, both of my sisters, and my brother walked in, looking at me standing next to Raven—me shirtless, covered in paint, with Raven standing wide-eyed and looking between us.

My mother grinned, my father raised a brow, and each of my siblings had a look that I didn't trust.

I held back a curse and pushed away from Raven, grateful that she could stand on her own.

Because the matchmaking Montgomerys knew no bounds, and this was a damn mistake.

In more ways than one.

Chapter 6

Raven

I HAD EATEN DINNER WITH THE MONTGOMERYS BEFORE. Multiple times while growing up. I even had dinner with Aria recently. But I hadn't had dinner with all of Sebastian's family as an adult.

It was awkward, and we hadn't even sat down to eat a bite yet.

"I so am loving your café, Raven," Tabby said with a smile.

I loved Tabby Montgomery. She was a kind woman, an organizer at heart just like I was, and got shit done. She kept the construction arm of Montgomery, Inc. together. Without her at the helm, I wasn't sure all of the businesses that the Montgomerys owned would be as connected and fruitful as they were. In fact, it was thanks to Tabby and Hailey working together that I even had this café with Greer.

"I'm just glad that you guys came. In fact, all of you have really helped out so much. I just hope that the place continues to at least have some business once the Montgomerys aren't the only customers."

Alex Montgomery, Sebastian's dad, rolled his eyes. "I'm pretty sure that the Montgomerys weren't your only customers. And anyone on this side of town now knows of a place to go. We've always had little cafés to stop by, but we like our pastries and our coffee."

"Just not as much as our cheese," Gus said.

Gus and his twin sister Dara were Sebastian and Aria's younger siblings. I wasn't sure how Alex and Tabby had been able to raise two sets of twins. I was an only child, but I could see the way the Montgomerys had worked as a unit with their children. Each family was different, and yet they were all there for each other. It was such a contrast when compared with how Marley's parents were. They were strict, unyielding, and it had taken every sweet word of mine and Marley's to even get Marley out of the house. Sebastian hadn't been part of that. Things were easier when Sebastian didn't come to Marley's house. Oh, they knew that Sebastian was part of our three musketeers, and later Sebastian and Marley were dating, but they hadn't liked it.

I don't know if I would've really relished the fact that my teenage daughter had gotten pregnant either, but I wouldn't have treated Marley and Sebastian that way. My parents were kind, but a little older, so they hadn't hung out with the Montgomerys much. They could have, as Sebastian's family would've always let them in, but they are a little more introverted. They were a major reason why I had moved back.

"I forgot about the cheese thing," I said after a moment, sipping my sparkling water.

I noticed that even though Sebastian, Aria, and I were over twenty-one, none of us were drinking. Then I remembered that there hadn't ever been alcohol in Sebastian's house. Alex Montgomery was a recovering alcoholic, and the kindest man I knew. He was open about it, and when we were teenagers and had snuck light beer—that was practically water—from a friend's older brother, he sat us down and explained about his past. I knew it wasn't all of it, because it wasn't my right to know, but he said that it was his job, as the father and uncle of so many members of the next generation, to make sure that we knew how to be responsible.

I had fallen a little bit in love with Sebastian's dad that day. Mostly because he was always kind to us, and the sweetest man imaginable.

"I can't believe you forgot about the cheese thing," Aria said with an eye roll. She nudged my arm, and I grinned.

"What? Not everybody needs cheese with every meal."

"Sacrilege," Dara said with a tease. Gus and Dara were around twenty now if I did my math right. Although I never could keep track of all of the siblings and cousins that were in their lives.

"We don't eat cheese with every meal. Plus, some of us have dairy allergies."

I turned to Sebastian, wide-eyed. "Really?"

He nodded. "I have to take a pill in order for me to enjoy cheese. I have no idea how that happened, but I feel like that's a sign of old age."

He grinned as he said it, and our gazes met, both of us swallowing hard and then looking away. I had to hope nobody noticed that because everybody was talking all at once about cheese and old age. But I didn't think that Aria had missed it.

I could not look at Sebastian that way. We were just friends, or we had been friends. Now we were strangers with this odd past between us I didn't want to think about.

I did not like Sebastian that way. I couldn't. I had stepped back in middle school the moment that Marley smiled at him like that and I found out she had had a crush on him too. Because Marley was sweet and quiet and if I had been in the way she would've walked away and let me have him. Even that thought made me laugh because Sebastian had never looked at me twice.

Not until the mudroom, and I was blaming the paint fumes.

Because there was no way Sebastian would be attracted to me.

"You'll notice that we do not have cheese at this meal," Tabby said primly, and I laughed.

"It's true. No cheese. Mostly because I'm pretty sure we'll have it tomorrow. It's not great for our cholesterol to indulge every day," Alex Montgomery said with a wink.

"Well, that's good. But now I'm craving it."

"See? One day you'll be just thinking about something normal, the next day you're face first into a head of cheese," Gus said with a laugh. "One of us, one of us."

I smiled.

As they all started discussing various family events coming up, I wanted to leave. I wanted to leave the moment that they had shown up and everything felt awkward. Because nothing had happened. Nothing was going to happen.

I didn't want this connection. I could not.

Because I was not one of them. Marley should have been one of them. It had been five years since she had died. Five years since Nora had come into our lives, and I had lost my best friend.

Maybe I had begun to lose her long before that because I had walked away, but there were reasons.

Reasons that didn't make any sense anymore. Reasons that made me feel selfish because I just wanted to be out of their shadow. Just be myself. Just to find myself.

Now I was back, and my parents needed me, and I had a job and friends and things were working out.

And all I could do was feel the heat of Sebastian beside me and the press of his leg against mine.

How could anyone miss this? This awkwardness?

I was doing everything wrong, and I needed to leave. But if I did, it would make it worse.

I ignored it as best I could and listened to Aria as she talked about her new job, and I answered questions about the café. I told them about pastry school and everything, while all I wanted to do was move my leg away. Sebastian's leg was just so damn big. Thick and muscled and I needed to stop thinking about him.

Maybe trying water again would help, so I took a big gulp.

"Okay, does it really take that many turns or whatever to make a croissant?" Dara asked, and I nodded, setting my glass down quickly. It sloshed over the floor, and I cursed, but then Sebastian was there, drying my hand. I pulled away as if he had burned me, and our gazes met.

I swallowed hard and he just raised a brow, that pierced brow, and I wanted to reach out and slap him upside the head. Or kiss him.

No, that would be bad. Oh, so bad. What was wrong

with me? I had never had this problem before. I was always good at holding back this reaction.

Maybe I was just too tired. After all, we had been really stressed out recently, and I hadn't had much sleep. Yes, that must be it.

"You okay?"

"Sorry, just tired."

"Oh no, you must work baker's hours, and we've been keeping you. I'm sorry," Tabby said gently.

I shook my head, even though I had literally just thought that I wasn't sleeping enough.

"No, really, I'm a dork. But I am much better at baking. And yes, you want to laminate the layers with any pastry like that, so you have to fold the dough over butter."

"Oh, I watch Bake Off. I know," Dara said with a sage nod.

I laughed. "Okay then."

"So why did you ask?" Gus asked, rolling his eyes at his twin.

"Now I want a croissant," Aria said with a happy sigh.

"Well, you are speaking to the right person. And yes, there'll be fresh croissants in the morning at the café."

"Look at you, making business."

"Like I'm going to make you pay."

"Damn straight you're going to make her pay," Gus growled.

He sounded so much like his brother then that I blinked.

"We Montgomerys each pay our own way. We don't take handouts," Sebastian said quietly from my side.

I swallowed awkwardly. "I know. I was just teasing. Of course, I'm going to make Aria pay. And double just because she annoys me." I tried to make light of it, as Aria laughed and the others joined in. But something looked off with Sebastian, and I didn't know what it was.

Or maybe I did, and I didn't want to think about it.

"Hey, Sebastian? I brought a few things for Nora. Is it okay if I just put them in her room?" Aria asked helpfully.

Everybody froze, as if the reason for Nora's absence wasn't why they were all there. Of course, they were there to comfort Sebastian on the weekend that he didn't have his daughter.

Just like I was. Though I still didn't know how that had all come about.

"What did you get her? You know I don't want to spoil her."

Aria rolled her eyes in the way of sisters. "I'm her favorite auntie, of course I'm going to spoil her."

"Excuse me, I'm literally sitting right here," Dara said quickly.

"And I'm Sebastian's twin. I'm sorry, that's just the way things are."

The girls begin to play fight, and I knew it was to

keep Sebastian's mind off Nora's absence, but all I could do was look at him, and wonder what the hell I was supposed to say. And why I was even there. I shouldn't be. I should be long gone, not part of this.

"You know, I do work baker's hours, so I should be going. But thank you for dinner. Seriously. I was just going to heat up some leftovers, if I even have leftovers in the fridge."

"I bet you always have baked goods though," Alex put in.

I smiled. "If I'm not testing out something, then you know there's something wrong. So yes," I said as I looked over at Sebastian. "Any time you need baked goods, come on over." It was only after I said the words that I realized it sounded like a come-on. Or maybe I was looking too deep into it.

I really needed to go.

I pushed back my chair and stood up quickly. "Thank you, seriously. I can cook okay, but I'm a better baker. And this was all amazing."

"It's just good to see you," Tabby said as she stood up and hugged me. I hugged her right back, that familiar feeling making me want to cry for some reason.

"It's good to see all of you."

"Sebastian, walk her to her house," Tabby ordered, and Sebastian pushed back from the table without saying a word.

Alarmed, I waved them off. "I live next door. It's still

somewhat daylight out. I'm fine. I walked over here on my own, I can leave on my own."

Although I hadn't really wanted to mention the fact that I had been here alone with Sebastian. It shouldn't matter. We were just friends. I was not Marley.

At that thought, ice-cold water slid through my veins.

Tabby just stared at me, and then back at her son.

And I knew whatever I said wasn't going to matter. They weren't going to let me walk home alone.

They all began to clean up.

"Come on," Sebastian said gruffly, and I swallowed hard and grabbed my phone. I hadn't even brought my bag over. It was lucky that I had even locked the door on my way out and that was the only reason I had my keys.

"I'm really okay," I said as we walked side by side through his backyard to mine. Our backyards were connected through a gate. I had found that weird at first, but now it was nice. Mostly so we had an easy walk between our two entrances rather than having to walk around the long windy driveways from our front doors.

"Thanks for doing that. My parents worry about me. I'm fine. I really am. I know where my kid is, I know she's safe." He paused. "Because if she isn't safe, I'm going to burn the whole world down."

I turned to him, both of us standing underneath the tree that covered both our yards. "Marley's parents aren't the nicest people, but they would never hurt Nora."

"Not physically, no. But if they hurt her emotionally? I can't really do much. The courts made me do the weekends. So I deal with it."

Without thinking I reached out and pushed his hair back from his face. We both froze at the action, and I swallowed hard, staring at those blue eyes of his.

They were like light oceans, beckoning me, and I knew that I was in so much fucking trouble.

"I should go," I whispered.

"You really should." He paused, swallowed hard. I refused to watch the way his throat worked. "My parents need to take care of me, same as my family. It's how it's always been. Thanks for being there so they didn't act awkward, like they were trying to make things light and happy when I didn't want them to be. But I'm sorry you were forced into it."

"I could have said no. I could have run away."

"Could you?" he asked, his voice low.

His gaze went to my lips and I couldn't help it, my tongue peeked out and I licked them. And then he swallowed hard again, his eyes going dark.

I hadn't realized his eyes could do that.

I stepped back, the moment breaking, and turned on my heel and ran.

I didn't say goodbye, I ran like a coward, because I wanted to kiss him. I wanted to do the one thing I shouldn't.

To kiss my best friend's boyfriend.

My dead best friend.

There were lines, lines so set in stone that they would break anyone who crossed them. And I refused to be broken. I refused to do that.

And I refused to be attracted to Sebastian Montgomery.

Chapter 7

Sebastian

I HAD ONCE AGAIN WOKEN UP WITH A HARD-ON FROM hell. Ever since realizing Raven was back, all my dick could do was get hard for her, and I didn't fucking understand it. I didn't want Raven like that. Right?

It didn't matter though, because my dick did. And apparently it had a mind of its own. I was going to have to strangle the thing.

That made my lips twitch. I would have strangled it, more than once. I was pretty sure that my left hand was now my girlfriend because it was the only thing ever touching my dick. And the only thing that would.

I did not *want Raven*. I just wanted the *idea* of her.

Because yes, she was hot. She had always been beautiful. But now she was *hot*, and I was attracted to her. I was allowed to be attracted to other people. Marley and I had always checked out other people together and laughed over the people we each found hot. Our taste was quite similar. So, me finding other people attractive wasn't new. But I wasn't going to act on it. I was allowed to. I'd had sex in the past five years. It hadn't been easy to let myself go to even do that, and every time it had been for one night, no promises, no strings, and I'd never see the person again. But this was different. Because this was Raven. I wasn't allowed to want her. I wasn't allowed to kiss her.

And yet I came thinking about her.

I'd slid my hand over my dick, squeezed hard, and then pumped into my fist, whacking off like a teenage boy, thinking of one of my former best friends, until I came hard. Hard enough that my knees nearly gave out, and I growled out Raven's name. Come had spurted on the bathroom wall, the water washing it away.

I kept coming thinking of Raven. How was I supposed to look her in the eye whenever I got coffee, knowing that I had wrung one out for her?

No, she never needed to know that. And I should stop doing it. I had control over my own dick. Over my own erections. I could do this.

And if I kept lying to myself, maybe it would become the truth.

"Hey, why are you staring off into space?" Tristan asked, and I looked over at my fellow tattoo artist.

He and his wife Taryn had the back two rooms of the shop and tried to work together as much as possible. I wasn't sure I would ever be able to work with anyone I was sleeping with, let alone married to, although I worked with all of my family, so I couldn't really talk. They fought as often as they made up, but the two worked well together, and they were both damn good artists.

"Sorry, I have no idea what I was thinking about."

"Sounds about right," the other man said with a laugh. "Seriously though, you want to talk about it?"

I shrugged. "Not really. I have a client coming in."

"We all do. It's damn good, isn't it?" he asked as he came over.

"Yeah. I am happy that we all seem to have a good client list, with only a few slots open for walk-ins."

"I like the walk-ins," Taryn said as she slid up to her husband. He wrapped his arms around her shoulders without even looking at her, the two of them in sync as always.

"What do you mean?" I asked, pushing that odd jealous thought from my mind. I didn't want what they had. I'd had that. And now I didn't, and I didn't have time for anything more. Maybe I could have a little heat, a little fun, but Nora was my number one priority, and then the shop. Nothing else mattered.

Again, another lie.

Taryn grinned. "I like being able to work on a small piece with somebody, on which they've already done their research, or when they just want something for fun that will remind them of a key moment in their life. Not everything has to be overly complicated and take a whole day. Sometimes it's a tiny little mark on their wrist to showcase a moment that they will always want to remember. It's fun."

I shook my head. "True. As long as you don't get the drunk frat guys."

She rolled her eyes. "Oh. I don't deal with them."

"Damn straight you don't. None of us do. They look drunk or belligerent? They're out of here."

I grinned at her. "It helps that you're a big bruiser of a man, even bigger than me, and could probably carry them out with one pinky."

Tristan flexed and Taryn rolled her eyes.

"That's my big man," she teased, and I gave a mock shudder.

"I really don't need to know."

Tristan grinned. "Oh yeah. Talk to me how you like it, wifey."

He leaned down and pressed his lips to hers, and I ignored that familiar jealousy.

Everyone around me was married, getting married, or having kids. I had the kid, I was doing good. I was fine.

And if I kept telling myself that, I would eventually believe it.

"Are they making out again?" Leo asked, and I shrugged at my friend and fellow tattoo artist.

"You're just jealous that May doesn't work here."

May was the manager of the local Montgomery Daycare Center and Nanny Services, as well as a teacher and provider for other nanny services around the country. She had been Leif's nanny for a while, and still was, though she ran the whole business now, too.

"I get to see my wife whenever I want." Leo beamed. "I just love saying my wife. It makes me feel all caveman."

"Damn straight," Tristan said as they fist-bumped.

"You know, it used to be that they would talk about the random women they were banging, and grunt and act all fake macho, and now they're here talking about china patterns and lace doilies."

"Did I mention a fucking china pattern?" Tristan asked, his voice going a little growly.

"You *are* the one who couldn't find his favorite mug yesterday."

"Because it was in a different place. And I like my special mug. You have your special bowl, the one that looks like a plate."

"It's called a pasta bowl. I don't know how many times I have to tell you," she teased, and the two began to bicker. It was practically foreplay for them. I didn't want to think about that.

"I'm going to go get some coffee," I said, seemingly randomly. But not random. Not even a little.

Because I needed to see Raven again.

She was my kryptonite, and I had no idea how that had happened.

Leo raised a brow. "Aren't you already caffeinated enough?"

"I haven't had anything from the café today. I brought in my own coffee."

"Are you going to get something sweet too?" Tristan asked, teasing.

I looked between them, frozen. "I could use a pastry."

"Sure," Leo added, drawing out the word.

"That's enough of that," I grumbled, grabbing my phone.

"Be nice. Although, Sebastian, if you're trying to hide that oddly growly way you get around her? Maybe you should stop going to the café as often as you do."

I turned to Taryn. "She's a friend. Always has been. And we all said we wanted to support their business, so that's what I'm doing."

I didn't mean to bite out the words like I had. She held up her hands in mock surrender, while Tristan glared at me.

I shrugged and moved past a grinning Noah who I hadn't even realized was in the doorway.

"You know, I could use some coffee too."

"Go back to your office." I snarled the words.

Noah wiggled his brows. "No, I don't believe I will. I'll be following." My cousin whistled as he walked past me and we went towards the café.

"Leave me the fuck alone," I grumbled.

"No, I won't. You know you could have gone through the side entrance. We did connect the two store-fronts for a reason."

"I needed the crisp cool air." I was such a damn liar.

"Probably to will down that erection of yours. Steel pipe, anyone?" Noah asked, his eyes dancing with laughter.

"Shove off."

"Hey. Don't get angry. This is cool. I like Raven. I like the way you two growl at each other and get all flustered."

"It's not—it's not like that. She's a friend."

"And she always has been. I know lying." He paused. "We like to razz you, but it's okay you know. You're allowed to look at other women."

"I'm not quite sure I need your permission," I whispered, before we walked inside.

"You don't. But maybe you need your own."

At that, Noah pushed past me, walking in first. "Greer, darling. Hook me up."

The barista laughed, shaking her head. "You're a menace. What are you in the mood for today?" she asked.

"You can't tell? I thought you were the psychic who always knew."

"I can, but you are so full of yourself sometimes I just don't even know."

"Ouch."

Others in the building laughed, everyone looking comfortable in tall chairs and comfy sofas. The place looked warm and inviting and though it looked as if some people were taking up real estate in their chairs, they were still eating and drinking. So the girls weren't losing money. That was good. I hadn't liked the other place. This needed to work. And not just for the Mont-gomerys. For Raven too.

I looked up to see Raven blinking at me.

"Hi. I'm just, well, I'm baking a cake. I'll be right back." She smiled at me, brushed flour from her cheek, and scrambled off to the back room.

Greer looked between us, brows raised.

"Well, I suppose I'll be getting your coffee order."

"Oh. Yeah." I looked down at my phone, which now had a slew of text messages.

"Apparently I'm getting coffee for the entire world here."

Noah looked over my shoulder. "I only have to get

mine, since everyone's out of the office today working on jobs."

"Oh?"

"Montgomery Security is doing well. Just like Montgomery Ink Legacy. Makes me happy."

"Damn straight. Okay, I have a few orders from the lazy asses next door who couldn't come over on their own."

Greer laughed and took my phone right out from my hands.

"I'll work on this, and it seems they want pastries, too. We've got you."

Raven came back from the kitchen and looked over Greer's shoulder.

"I'll help you. And we'll get this done quickly. I notice they just said sandwiches, but without telling me what they want. Do you know?"

I shook my head. "I have no clue," I said, and then she finally looked at me.

I swallowed hard, willing my dick to behave.

But it wasn't just that.

There was this tightness in my chest—I could breathe, but it was getting harder and harder to do. But this was *Raven*, I knew her. Why did it feel like this?

Thankfully she broke the eye contact first, to look over my phone again.

I stuck my hands in my pockets, awkward as hell.

"Um, just whatever you want. Maybe a variety? Or if that's too difficult, just do all the same thing."

Raven looked at me, brow raised. "I think I can handle a variety. I'll think of something fun."

"Don't go out of your way. I know you're busy."

She smiled sweetly and it went straight to my dick. Again. "And I can help my friends. Don't worry. Plus, I like coming up with interesting sandwiches."

Greer leaned forward. "Because whenever she gets to be creative with you guys, it goes on our menu, and everybody wins. Plus, I get to name them when she lets me."

"This cranberry turkey thing is amazing," a customer said, before he devoured his last bite.

My stomach rumbled. "I want what he's having," I teased, and Raven blushed. It was such a pretty blush.

"I can do that," she said in a rush and went back to work.

I stood next to Noah, who was shaking his head. "Okay, I've got my coffee, and now I need to get back to work. As interesting as this was, I really need to know how it ends."

I glared. "It's just coffee."

"Sure it is, brother. Sure it is." He tilted his drink at Greer, said his goodbyes, and sauntered out. There was really no other word for it.

My cousin saw way too fucking much. But then

again, I wasn't exactly hiding my attraction. I was usually better at this, why couldn't I this time?

By the time I paid for everything, and Greer stacked up the coffees, Raven came out, her arms full of food.

"Are you going to be able to get this all through on your own?"

"I can make trips."

Greer shook her head. "No, Raven can help you." Raven gave Greer such a dirty look that I had to hold back a smile.

Well, wasn't this interesting?

"Okay so I guess you are volunteering me?"

"I'm just saying," she sing-songed, and practically pushed Raven out from behind the counter.

"By the way, your door's locked on the other side, so you're going to have to go around the front."

I cursed under my breath. "Seriously?"

"Yep. Sorry, I know we did it so that way it was able to be locked on both sides, but we're going to have to have a system or something."

I nodded, making a mental note of that as I grabbed the coffees, and Raven grabbed the food.

"Thank you," I said as we walked outside.

"It's really okay. I don't mind."

We turned slightly and stood in front of the brick wall that separated the two glass windows. There was a gap so no one would be able to see from inside either place. I swallowed hard, knowing that if I didn't say something, it was going to be awkward as hell from now on. There was no denying it, no hiding it. There was an attraction here.

But I didn't know what to say. So instead, I latched onto something she had said before, something that was out of the blue, but worked.

"You should get some ink."

She raised her brows, eyes wide. "Sebastian."

"You want it, I'll do it. You can trust me."

She was quiet for so long, I knew that had probably come so far out of left field that she didn't know what to say.

"Trusting you with my body isn't the problem, Seb." Her eyes went wide, and a growl slipped from my lips.

"Stop it, Sebastian," she whispered.

"Not a chance." I leaned down and pressed my lips to hers. Our hands were full, so I couldn't do more. I slid my tongue along her lips and she parted them for me. She tasted of coffee and sweetness. We were standing in front of both of our businesses, hidden slightly, but not enough. So I pulled back, watched her cheeks pinken even more, and said the first thing that came to mind.

"Run with me."

Again, I was just blurting shit that didn't make any sense. I'd thought of it, sure, because I'd seen her run and loved the way she looked in her tight leggings. But I hadn't planned on saying the words aloud.

"What?"

"Run with me. I take Nora on runs all the time. It's fun. You should join us. It's something, you know?"

What the hell was I doing?

"Sebastian," she whispered.

"Just run with us. Or get a tattoo, or do something. I just, I know you feel it, too."

She pressed her lips together and nodded. "I do, fine. I'll go on that run. I don't know if I'm ready for a tattoo."

I nodded, and somehow piled the food on top of the coffees, without spilling or dropping any of it.

"I've got it from here. I'll see you soon."

She met my gaze, blinked, nodded, and turned and walked away.

I knew I was making a mistake. But this time it was one I was willing to make.

Chapter 8

Raven

"Why am I doing this again?" I asked no one as I pulled my hair to the top of my head and made a sort of bun thing.

I really shouldn't be doing this. In fact, I should be running in the opposite direction. But I didn't think I was going to have another option. Not when I had already said yes, and not when I really wanted to.

And that was on me. It was so stupid. It would be easier if I would just walk away, not run towards this. But I knew this wasn't a choice.

"Fucking get out of your head and just get it done."

That was enough of the pep talks today.

I slid my feet into my running shoes, happy I'd gotten the kinds without ties. I hated having to tie my shoes. Nora could probably tie her shoes better than I could at this point. I just loved slip-ons.

I slid my phone into the pocket of my leggings, once again grateful that companies started making those so I didn't have to strap my phone to various parts of my body.

When I opened the door, steeling myself for what was to come, I paused, surprised that they were already there.

"Raven! You're here! I'm so excited that you're going to be running with us. My legs are too short to run and Daddy doesn't like to push the stroller anymore because I'm a big girl, so now I have a bike." She pointed down to her brand-new bike, complete with bow and tassels.

I smiled. "Look at that. And you match your helmet."

I purposely didn't look behind Nora because I didn't want to see him.

"Daddy got it for me because I'm too big for my baby bike. I don't even need training wheels." She beamed and flicked her tongue against her loose tooth.

I held back my shudder, because I hated teeth. I hated the idea of loose teeth, cavities, drilling, anything having to do with the dentist. I had no idea how Sebastian dealt with a little girl who was about to lose all of the teeth inside her head and have those replaced by new ones. How was that normal?

"I see you're ready to go?" a deep voice said, interrupting my thoughts.

I turned to see him then and swallowed hard. He had on a soft, gray T-shirt that clung to his muscles. It was short sleeved so I could see most of his ink, and running shorts that stopped right above the knee. Whenever he lifted his leg, the shorts would ride up and I would be able to see more—and I should not think about that.

I shouldn't think about the fact that Sebastian had thick thighs, and I loved thick thighs. There was something wrong with me.

"Are you ready to go?" Nora asked, bouncing on her seat.

I nodded, then turned and locked the door, checking to make sure it was secure. "I'm ready. Should I have brought water or something?"

Sebastian pointed to Nora's bike. "It has space for two water bottles, so we can share. Or, I have money, we'll stop for a coffee or something."

"Can I have a coffee?" Nora asked, fluttering her little eyelashes.

Sebastian rolled his eyes. "When you're thirty."

"Sebastian, you're not even thirty yet."

He narrowed his eyes at me, and it did things to me that I didn't want to think about.

"Don't be a traitor."

"Rude," I teased, and he shook his head and rolled his shoulders back.

"You going to stretch at all?" he asked, his voice oddly deep.

I licked my lips, and his gaze tracked the movement. Oh God. This was going to be a problem. A very big problem. But I nodded and slowly bent down, stretching my legs a bit, paying attention to my thighs because I tended to get tight there.

I didn't bend down in front of him and was thankful that my sports bra and tank covered everything. The last thing I needed to do was flash Sebastian in front of his daughter.

I didn't need to flash Sebastian at all, I needed to remember that. I was not insane. But I sure as hell felt like it by then.

"Okay, ready?" Sebastian asked after a moment, his voice a deep growl.

"I'm ready, Daddy!" Nora called out, and then she pumped her little legs, and she was moving like fire.

"Oh. Am I supposed to catch up with her?" I asked, holding back my laugh.

Sebastian shook his head. "She'll slow down. She knows to stay on the same block as me, so I can always see her. Usually she just rides right next to me, and I try not to let her run into my ankles." He snorted. "I'll block you if she comes at us. She's decent at the bike, but it's still touch and go sometimes."

I couldn't help it, I laughed and shook my head. "This is going to be interesting."

He met my gaze for a long moment. "Interesting sure works."

We took off after Nora, with me running beside him. He was taller than me by more than a few inches, maybe even a foot. I had to work twice as hard to keep up with him, but I liked running. This was something I could do, and Sebastian didn't seem to want to talk right then, at least when he was keeping an eye on Nora, so I wouldn't have to pant every other word.

Because just making sure that my breathing didn't sound like I was suffocating was hard enough. I didn't know if I could make conversation.

We turned the corner and moved down the block towards the park. This neighborhood had wide sidewalks, and a biking path for Nora if needed. The speed limit was low, this area was made for families. There was even a coffee shop and a couple small stores for last-minute groceries at the entrance of the neighborhood. We weren't a big city, but it was still a place that you had to drive everywhere, though at least they thought about func-tionality when they planned the community. I appreciated it, and I was sure that Sebastian appreciated the safety of it. That was probably why the Montgomerys had built so many of the houses here. They did good work, steady work. One day, when I had the money and the inclination, I would buy a house that they made. Probably not a new one, but even their older ones were good quality.

Eventually Nora slowed down and wiggled between us. She only hit me once with the tire, and we nearly both went sprawling. Sebastian gripped Nora's shirt, keeping her steady, as I took a few stumbling steps, laughing.

"Well, you warned me," I said, sucking in a deep breath.

Sebastian shook his head and looked down at Nora. "What did we say about trying tricks?" he asked, teasing in his voice.

"That I should wait until I'm with the uncles so you can blame them?" she asked, her humor so much like her father's that it sent me back in time.

Sebastian had always been the funny one, I was the quiet, steady one, Marley was the shy one. We had all worked together, egging each other on, as best friends do.

I didn't know when exactly that all changed, maybe when I backed away from wanting to share my lunch with Sebastian at the lunch table, since I knew Marley wanted to. Or that she wanted to hold his hand when we went to the retro roller-skating rank.

I had walked away. And I hadn't let myself dive deep into that little crush. Not until I came back. And boy did it feel like such an odd betrayal even though it shouldn't. Even though it couldn't be.

"You good?" he asked, and I nodded. "I'm fine. I'm not hurt, as long as Nora's fine."

"I'm good. Sorry. I got a little loose."

I frowned, trying to figure out what she meant by that, but Sebastian nodded.

"She wasn't holding onto the handlebars as tightly," he clarified.

I nodded. "Oh. That makes sense. You ready to begin again?"

"Yeah. Do you need coffee or something?"

I shook my head, afraid of spending too much time with them. It felt a little too nice. And I didn't want to think too hard about it. "I don't know if you know, but my best friend and former roommate makes coffee for a living. I can't cheat on her."

I paused, the word 'cheat' feeling weird. This wasn't cheating. Sebastian wasn't with anyone.

But there was a ghost between us. I couldn't let myself forget that.

Sebastian just grinned. "You're right, it would feel wrong. Although I do drink coffee at Taboo when I'm visiting my dad. Sorry."

"Considering Hailey owns part of our business, and we're her franchise, I think Taboo's fine." I laughed.

"That makes sense. Nora loves the hot cocoa there."

"Hailey's the best." Nora beamed. "But I want to try yours, too. Who's your best friend?"

"Her name is Greer. I think you'd love her."

"I'm sure I will," Nora said. "Besides, Molly and Shane said I need to keep making friends so that way we have a big group like my daddy does."

"Molly and Shane are your best friends?" I asked, feeling an odd sense of déjà vu.

She nodded, playing with the tassel on her bike.

"Yep. We all like to draw, but Molly and Shane say I'm the best. I love to read, too, and so do they. And we can even read big kid books. And then we're also in soccer and dance, but I think Molly's going to be better at dance, or maybe Shane. I'm not as good at dance as I am soccer. I'm a sweeper."

She kept talking, going a mile a minute, and I just shook my head, smiling.

She was so much like Marley in that moment. Because Marley was shy, until she was with her best friends, then she blurted out everything.

History had a way of repeating itself, and it was odd. And yet, warm.

I looked up at Sebastian, meeting his gaze, and I knew he was thinking the exact same thing, remembering the same memories. But it didn't hurt this time. I didn't know why I was on this run, why I had let him kiss me, why I wanted more. I still wanted more. And I didn't know what I was going to do with that.

Eventually we started our run again, Nora was getting tired, and because I had had to run double pace to keep up with them, I was a little tired too. When we made our way back to the houses, we stood in the front porch area, laughing, and Sebastian brought me out coffee.

"It's not Greer's, but it's decent."

"You know what, it sounds amazing. And thanks for the bottle of water, too."

"No problem. Got to stay hydrated."

"Do you want to do it again? Not today, because we have things to do and I know you're not supposed to overwork yourself, but I love my bike. And you're pretty. And you can run. I like running." Nora continued to talk, and I just laughed.

"Yes. That would be fun." I blurted the words, thinking of Nora, but when I looked at Sebastian, he had a small smile on his face.

He wasn't saying no, wasn't saying this was too much, or too weird.

Well then.

Somebody pulled into the driveway then, and I knew from the way Sebastian's shoulders tensed and how he set down his mug, that something was going to be bad. This wasn't one of the countless Montgomerys.

I turned around and saw a familiar couple getting out of a Buick. I knew them even though it had been a few years since the funeral. The woman glared at me and looked between us, I knew what she saw.

A man and a woman and a child laughing and drinking coffee in the morning on a front porch. I saw the tableau and it didn't matter that I might want Sebastian, that Nora was already a light in my life, I wasn't Marley.

"Unfaithful," Marley's mother snapped. "How could you do this? How could you do this to my daughter? Who is this woman? This tramp? Why is she near Nora? You let this woman sleep in your bed when my granddaughter is right beside her?"

I froze, setting my coffee cup down next to Sebastian's, appalled.

Marley's parents had always been tightly wound and conservative in what they thought their daughter should be. But they had never been this bitterly acidic before. At least not to me.

I reached out and slid my hand over Nora's head unconsciously, and she wrapped her arms around my waist, burying her face into my stomach. I held her close, wanting to shield her.

Marley's mother continued to spew hate as Marley's father glowered behind her.

These were Nora's *grandparents*.

I had no idea what to say. I wanted to reach out and shake them, to tell them that there was still a little girl here. Theirs might be gone, but Nora was innocent in all of this. How could they treat her like this?

"Raven, please take Nora inside." His voice was so calm, so cool.

He was holding back everything for his daughter. Because this was already a scene, and he didn't want to make it worse.

I nodded, meeting his gaze. I tried to will my thoughts to him, for him to know that I stood by him, that I wasn't going to let Nora get hurt. But I didn't even know if he could see me right then, not with the pain that Marley's parents slammed at us.

I turned, taking Nora with me as I walked inside. The fact that she went so easily with me and without even needing her daddy worried me. I moved her back, so I could brush her hair from her face.

"It's okay, baby."

Tears streaked her little cheeks, and I reached for a tissue, wiping them away. "Why do they make my dad so sad?" Nora asked, still crying.

It felt like something had lashed my heart, because Nora wasn't worried about her own feelings. She was worrying about her daddy. I hated all of this. I didn't know what to say, but I knew I needed to say something.

"They just miss your mom and they're not very good at saying what they need to. But none of what they say is about you. You're such a good girl."

"But I killed my mom."

She said the words so softly, so matter-of-factly, that they took a second to register. I was already kneeling in front of her, so when I fell on my butt, I took her with me, clinging her to me.

"What? No, you didn't, baby. You didn't."

"But I did. I was born and she died. And Grandma always says God has a plan, but I don't like the plan since that means my mom is dead."

I pressed my lips together, so angry and so out of my depth. I wasn't good at this. I wasn't good at any of this, but I needed to be. Sebastian wasn't here, he was dealing with Nora's grandparents. This wasn't my place, yet what was I supposed to do? Walk away when this little girl was hurting?

"I'm not good at this, Nora. I don't know why your mom isn't here, and I don't think it's fair. But you did not kill her. I don't want you to ever use those words again because you didn't hurt her. I don't know about plans or what was supposed to happen, but it's not fair. Your mom and your dad were my best friends. I hate that she's not here. But you know what? You look so much like her, Nora. You even remind me of her. So she's here, inside of you." I put my hand over her little heart, as she looked up at me with wide eyes. "I knew her when we were your age. And she was so sweet. I'm sorry so darn sorry that she's not here. But I'm glad that your dad is here for you. Because he's so great. He loves you. And he doesn't blame you."

I hadn't heard the door, but as it snicked closed I turned and saw him there, anger etched on his face before he blinked it away, to be replaced by an odd look, and I knew he had heard all of it. Every single word.

He knelt between us, kissed the top of Nora's head, and then kissed my forehead.

Okay then.

I had no idea what I was supposed to do about that.

"Come on. Let's make some chocolate pancakes, and then I do believe Nora has some art to show us."

Nora looked up at him and smiled. "I love you, Daddy."

"I love you, munchkin."

"Daddy," she said, exasperated.

"I love you, my Nora. And I love your mom too." He kissed her forehead again, and then stood up, taking his daughter with him. He held out his hand to help me off the floor.

Yes, he loved Marley, but he was a different man now. Things were different. Because I loved Marley too, I didn't know what to do.

I looked up at him. "Sebastian." So many questions in that one word, and I didn't have answers.

"Just stay, Raven. We can make our own rules."

I slid my hand into his and knew that was the problem.

Chapter 9

Sebastian

MAKE OUR OWN RULES.

Make our own rules.

I'd actually said those words to Raven. That we were going to make our own rules and do what we wanted.

It wasn't just chocolate pancakes and sketching with Nora. It wasn't holding back the rage from hearing my daughter say she had killed her mother. It couldn't be any of that.

My hands fisted at my sink as I struggled to calm down.

That night I had tucked my daughter into bed and

held her just like Raven had when she talked about Marley.

I had loved Marley. She would always hold part of my heart. The person I had been when I was with Marley might be gone, but that didn't matter. Because no matter where I went in my future, she was part of it. She was my past, and Nora's mother.

I didn't know if I wanted to love again, or have a relationship. I didn't know if that was in the cards for me, but I also knew I was in my early twenties, and every time one of my cousins said that they were never going to do anything like that, one slapped them upside the head so hard that they couldn't function.

I wasn't going to be that idiotic. But I also wasn't going to go all-in at the first chance.

Apparently, making our own rules meant going to dinner together.

I had point-blank asked Raven to dinner, and she had said yes, but I wasn't sure she knew she had done so. We had sort of just mumbled to each other.

I hadn't kissed her again, though I wanted to. But we had Nora between us, and I had wanted to spend the afternoon with Nora to make sure that she understood that what her grandparents said wasn't right. And that Nora was so special, and her mother loved her so much, even from heaven.

Even though saying that had torn something out of me.

But here I was, standing in dark jeans and finishing shaving my face.

I usually had a big beard, but I had taken to shaving it down so it was just a little bit of stubble. Nora liked it that way, and whatever my little girl wanted, she got.

I was losing my damn mind. But I also knew that I needed to move on. I needed to look toward a future where I didn't hate myself and didn't make my daughter question things. Maybe Marley's parents yelling the way they had pushed me into something that I wasn't sure I was ever going to do. But that didn't matter.

I liked Raven. We were friends for years, and while I hadn't seen her any other way because I had been with Marley, there was something there now, and I was going to lean into it.

Or lose my mind.

"Knock knock," a familiar voice said from my bedroom, and I quickly wiped off my face and padded out to see my twin standing there, brows raised.

"Auntie Aria is here to babysit. Nora is in her room drawing and humming to herself, so I thought I would come in here and bug you."

I sighed and pulled a Henley over my head.

"So, where are you taking our girl?" Aria asked as she leaned against the dresser.

"Just to Henry's."

Aria nodded, smiling. "It's a good place." A pause. "It's a family place."

"I don't think Henry's is actually owned by a Montgomery, but for all I know a family member's friend or cousin or brother-in-law owns it." I paused and looked at my twin. "Do they?"

Aria snorted. "No, but it's a family place in the sense that we go there a lot. One of our family members could be there for dinner."

I paused in the act of putting on my watch. "I didn't think about that. Just knew it was a good place and I liked the food. It's reasonably priced, and it popped up after Raven moved away so she hasn't been there. I didn't think about family." I grumbled that last part.

"I can put an alert out into the group chat. I don't want to hit the mega group chat because that's scary with over one hundred of us on it, but we could start the spiderweb."

My lips twitched and I shook my head. We had multiple group chats—the immediate family, just the kids in our immediate family, and then with our cousins, second cousins, et cetera. In fact, we went by geography in some cases. There was one that had every single family member, including my grandparents, but we didn't use that often. Mostly because the cacophony of noise and notifications from that got insane. It was for emergencies, and everybody knew not to reply directly unless they had something to say.

"No need. If we see them there, we see them there.

It's not like I can hide the fact that I'm going on a date with Raven, considering I asked you to babysit Nora."

"I would babysit Nora if you wanted to go sit out on the porch and just breathe. I love that little girl."

I smiled hard. "I know you do. We wouldn't be here without you."

"I'm the best aunt in the world, I know. And if you tell any of our aunts I said that, I will hurt you. Or our sister. Please don't tell her."

I snorted, thinking of our younger sister. "She could break you. You're strong, but she's stronger."

"I hate the fact that you're probably right. And, before I walked in here, I was going to say I couldn't believe you're going out on a date with Raven, but thinking about the way you two seem to be near each other, it fits."

I slid my feet into my shoes and frowned. "How do you think it fits? You've rarely seen us together."

"I have enough. You work next to each other, and I have my ways."

"You work on the other side of us."

"Okay, that's right. Seriously though, I don't know. You guys act weird around each other, as if you're trying to ignore the subtle tension that's there now. I know there was nothing going on between you when you were with Marley."

I whirled on her, my eyes narrowed. "Seriously?"

She held up her hands. "I just said I knew there was

nothing. Stop it. All I'm saying is that I'm happy for you."

"It's just a date."

"And it's not just a hookup. I know you've hooked up in the past few years. You're allowed to. Hell, I've hooked up with people."

I pinched the bridge of my nose. "We are twins. We shared a womb. We don't need to share this."

"Fine. But I just wanted to say I love you, and I like Raven, so I hope it all goes well. Whatever well it means. I know you are going to be careful." She paused. "I meant with each other's emotions and hearts, but be careful the other way too. Well, because, you know, your track record and all."

"Aria. Stop it. I'll have you know I've always used a condom."

What was left unsaid was they didn't work all the time. But I didn't want to dwell on that. Because I couldn't. My daughter was alive because of a broken condom. Marley was dead because of a broken condom. But I wasn't going to dwell on that.

"Okay, go pick her up, and I will take care of Nora."

"You know, I trust you with my little girl. No matter what happens. I trust you."

For some reason, her eyes filled, and I held back a curse.

"There's no need for you to cry. Didn't mean for you to cry."

"I love you, big bro."

My lips twitched. "Those few minutes really count, don't they?"

"You know they do. Now, have fun and make good choices."

"Fuck off, little sister."

"No, I do not believe I will."

She pushed me out the door. I shook my head, letting her. She was strong, but I was stronger, I could have stopped her if I wanted to.

I popped into Nora's room and tried my best to say goodbye, but she was entranced by her drawing, as her audiobook read her a Percy Jackson story.

I frowned, then remembered it was just the first one so she wouldn't be too scared.

"Don't let her go to the second one without us in the room," I called to Aria.

"She's tough, but we'll do it together. Now go. Have fun."

I headed out and awkwardly walked across the path to Raven's house.

Her doorbell alert must have caught me on camera before I could even knock, and she was already there, standing in leather pants, a flowy top, and high silver heels.

I wanted to reach out and slide my fingers down the leather just to see what they felt like, but I refrained. Only just.

"Hell."

Her lips twitched. "Oh?"

"You look sexy. And it's really hard for me not to lean forward and kiss you and try to gently convince you to go back into your house." I cursed under my breath. "Hadn't meant to say that out loud. I'm trying to be casual here, not creepily aggressive."

She laughed, a sound that warmed me from the inside out. There was something seriously wrong with me.

"You are very good for my ego. And I was just thinking that your jeans hug your ass quite nicely, and I just wanted to reach out and feel it. I think it's the amount of coffee that Greer has been pouring through my system that did that."

I grinned. "Sounds like a fucking plan. However, let's go on a date, though I'm not good at dating."

She raised her brow. "Really?"

I shrugged, slid my hands in my pockets. "I haven't really dated before."

There was a brief silence between us, but Raven nodded, her smile soft. "You know, that makes sense. You and Marley went straight from sharing each other's crayon box to finding your way past the whole awkward dating conversations of middle school and high school. And I assume anything since have been hookups?"

She was so matter of fact about it, I knew she pushed herself to say it, but damn if it wasn't sexy. And it relieved the tension between us, because Marley was always going to be there. We couldn't hide from it, but if we talked about it, maybe it wouldn't be so awkward. Or maybe it would be just awkward enough that it wouldn't hurt as much.

"Pretty much. And I'm not in middle school anymore." I paused at her laughter. "I don't want just a casual hookup." I blurted the last part, and her eyes widened.

"I don't know what I want, Sebastian." But before I could say anything, she continued. "But I'm not good at casual, and I don't want just a hookup. We were friends first. You can't just be a casual hookup when you have over a decade of friendship behind you."

"Damn straight. Now, let's go to Henry's."

"Greer told me it was amazing," she said as we walked back over to my car.

"Really, she's been there?" I asked, after we got in. We made our way down the road, music soft background noise, the scent of her filling the inside of my car. It was hard to think, but I was going to have to if I was going to make it through the evening.

"She hasn't gone, but Noah and Ford told her. It really is like being in college and living in a dorm with all of you guys, with the security staff in one section, the café and tattoo shop, and then Wyatt next door."

"Wyatt may not be a Montgomery, but he hangs out with us enough he might as well be."

"He doesn't hang out with you at night?" she asked.

"He has a couple of times, but he has his own friends. Hell, even Ford doesn't hang out with us every day, even though he and Noah are roommates and best friends. We do sometimes have friends outside of the Montgomerys. Shocking. I know."

"True, and Wyatt has that new girlfriend, Cora, that he's been bringing around. She's gorgeous, and it looks like he's flat-out in love with her."

"Good for him. He's been talking about wanting something like that since I've known him."

"And shockingly, he isn't dating a Montgomery. You would think with the high percentage of you in the area, that's like winning the lottery."

"Were you always this sarcastic?" I asked as we made our way inside.

"Yes. But I feel like my sarcasm's gotten a little snarkier? Or maybe we just know enough of each other from before that it all ties together."

"Tell me about what's happened since you moved. I want to hear about college. About opening this bakery."

Raven smiled as we took our seats. "And I want to know too." She paused. "We don't have to talk about the sad stuff tonight. But I'd love to talk about opening up Montgomery Ink Legacy, and college, and all of that."

"Did you like college?" I asked, figuring out this new Raven. Because she wasn't the same as before. But I wasn't that Sebastian either.

We ordered our drinks and our appetizer came out, along with a familiar face who sat down at the next table, and I looked over to see Wyatt beaming at us.

"This is a coincidence," Wyatt said with a smile. He looked at Raven and nodded. "Nice to see you. This is Cora," he said, gesturing to his girlfriend.

She had dark brown hair, with a few red streaks, and a bright smile.

"I'm so happy to finally meet you guys. I know I've seen you in passing, but you've always been so busy that I didn't want to interrupt."

"It's nice to meet you, too," I said at the same time as Raven.

"Well look at this, it's like we're on a double date," Wyatt said with a wink, and I rolled my eyes, as Raven blushed and Cora clapped her hands.

"I promise we're not going to bother you. Well, I am probably going to eavesdrop and bother you because I just love watching people dating. All the romance of it, it's like my own personal romcom."

Wyatt leaned forward and gripped her hand. "We can live our own romcom too, babe."

"Aww."

I met Raven's gaze, but she just pressed her lips together, trying not to laugh.

We were not a romcom, we were not a movie. But we were figuring it out.

They ordered their drinks and we settled in to eat our appetizer, and we ended up having a double date.

And afterwards, I felt lighter than I had in a long while.

Tonight just felt good, and though I hadn't seen another Montgomery, having Wyatt and Cora there while we all got to know each other opened up more parts of ourselves I hadn't expected.

"I didn't know that you got a minor and a major," Raven said as she leaned against the chair, our leftovers in her lap.

"I wanted to make sure that I had art, and not just what I taught myself or my family taught me. I had taken classes of course, but I wanted more. And I wanted the business degree because I knew I wanted this to be an actual business, and not me riding on the coattails of my family." I hadn't meant to say that last part, but Raven nodded.

"I know what you mean. You guys are a legacy, it is a lot to live up to. At least on the outside in. It's hard to get into the Montgomery family dynamic."

I pulled into Raven's driveway, turned off the car, and turned to her. "We are a cult. We literally open our doors for everyone. I've never heard that it's hard to be friends with us…"

Her eyes widened and she shook her head. "That's not it. It's more that you guys are intimidating. In a good way. You are just so open and always there for each other. And while my parents are sweet and amazing and caring, they are older, and I didn't have siblings. I went from a tiny little close-knit family, to this big world on the periphery of you guys. I loved it, don't get me wrong. But it is a different dynamic."

"We're not too much for you?" I asked, as I leaned forward and brushed my finger along her jaw.

She licked her lips, and I went hard as a rock.

"Oh, I wouldn't say that."

"I'm going to kiss you now. Is that okay?"

"I've been really hoping you would all night."

I groaned, then I leaned down and brushed my lips along hers. I wanted more, and I could barely hold back, my hand on her jaw, deepening the kiss as our tongues brushed against one another.

She slid her hand up my chest and up my neck, to curl into my hair, the kisses deepening, until we broke apart, our breaths coming in pants.

"Holy hell, you're addicting."

"I was going to say the same." She swallowed hard, and I watched the way that her lips moved, all swollen from my touch.

"Do you need to go inside now?" she asked, her voice low.

I looked down at my watch and shook my head. "I have some time."

My cock pressed against my zipper, and I knew that

wasn't what she was asking. My time wasn't always my own, but for now it could be.

"Come inside my place? Aria's going to look outside and know. I don't care, but what do you think?"

I nodded, grateful I parked in front of her place.

"She won't be able to see the car right away, but I'll text her, in case she's worried."

"Just come inside, Sebastian."

She slid out of the car, and I watched her walk towards her door, confident, her hips rolling in those leather pants.

I willed myself to breathe, then texted my sister I would be a little while longer.

When she sent a winking emoji and told me to stay the night, I cursed under my breath, and shoved my phone into my pocket, and did my best not to run after Raven.

A slight jog would do well enough.

As soon as the door closed behind me, I grabbed Raven's hand and crushed my mouth to hers. I should probably slow down, or do something more, but I didn't want to drink, I didn't want desserts. I just wanted Raven. When she slid her hands underneath my Henley and dug her nails into my skin, I rocked against her.

"I just, I just need you. Okay?" she whispered, and I nodded then pressed her back against the door.

We continued to kiss, our hands roaming all over one

another, and then I did what I wanted to do this whole evening and run my hands down her leather pants.

I groaned and took a step back so I could look at her.

"Those fucking pants are painted on. I love them."

She blushed. "Greer told me to wear them. But now I'm worried they're going to be a little hard to get off."

I swallowed hard. "Oh, I'll get you off."

She laughed, just like I wanted her to. I pulled at her pants and went down to my knees.

She slid out of her heels and I pulled her pants over her very luscious ass.

I groaned. "So fucking beautiful."

I kept pulling at them until she was in just her panties and that flowy top of hers. I stood back up and tugged on her hair, her mouth parted, and I used that action to crush my mouth to hers.

I slid my hand under her panties, cupping her. She gasped, the movement quick, but she was hot and wet already, so I slid my fingers between her lower lips, swollen, so wet, but I didn't fuck her with my finger. Instead, I just teased and I slid my hand back out.

Eyes wide, her lips parted, and I gently pressed my middle finger to her lip. I was coated in her wetness, just from that brief touch, and her tongue darted out to taste herself.

"So fucking sexy."

I tugged on her top, and she put her hands up so I could easily slide the shirt off her.

Soon she was just in her bra and panties, while I was still fully dressed, and I let my eyes get their fill of her.

"I'm going to fuck you hard and make you come. What do you say?"

"I say you're all talk and no cock."

I burst out laughing, which made her blush, so I quickly undid her bra, her breasts filling my hands as the lace fell to the ground.

"Sebastian!" she panted.

I played with her nipples, squeezing, twisting, before I leaned down and took one nipple in my mouth. I continued to suck, to bite, pleasuring her with just that touch. My free hand went down between her thighs, playing with her over her panties.

She rubbed against me, her back pressed against the door, and I swallowed hard, needing more.

I went to kneel down, but realized she was so short that it was going to be awkward, so I quickly gathered her up in my arms.

"Dear Lord. How do you move so fast?"

"My cock is like a steel rod right now, and I think I'm going to break. If I don't move quickly, I'm going to come in my jeans."

"That would be a problem," she said, wide-eyed, all innocent like.

There was nothing innocent about her in that moment, and I was fucking happy about it.

I set her on the edge of the couch and tugged on her panties.

"Now, let me have my dessert."

"You're still dressed."

"Yes? And I'm going to have my face in this pussy right now."

Before she could say anything, I spread her thighs, told her to hold on tight, and I slid my tongue along her wetness.

She was pink and wet and slick. She gasped my name when I sucked on her. I spread her, watching the way that she pulsed in front of me. She was luscious and sweet and a little tart, and when I slid one finger deep inside her, she came.

Just like that, and I had to reach up to grip her hips so she wouldn't fall back on the couch.

Her thighs clamped around my shoulders, and I grinned, continuing to suck and lick.

When I stood up, she was wet and flushed and shaking.

"I've never come that fast in my life."

"That sounds like a reward for me." I tugged on her hair again, arching her neck back as I kissed her.

When her hand slid to my belt, I moved back and helped her undo my belt, then my pants. She slid her hand beneath my boxer briefs, her eyes wide.

"I didn't know you were pierced."

I grinned and shoved my shoes off and my pants down below my ass.

"I have a lot of things pierced."

She slid her finger gently over the hoop at the tip of my dick, eyes wide. "Wow. That's going to…"

"It's going to feel real fucking good." I paused. "I have a condom. One that'll work with this. I have it on me because, well, I know exactly what happens when condoms break."

I didn't blush as I said it, it was reality.

Raven nodded. "I'm clean, I have an IUD, but I'm really fucking grateful that you have a condom."

"Good to know."

But before I could do anything but strip off my shirt, Raven slid to her knees and enveloped my cock with her mouth. The piercing hit the back of her throat, and she gagged a bit, before she slid her head back. "Wow. A girl could chip a tooth," she teased.

"I'll be gentle. I promise." I paused. "This time."

Her eyes darkened with need. I slid my hand in her hair and gently pressed her face back to my dick. When she opened her mouth, I slowly fucked her, going in and out, loving the way that she melted for me. I was dominant in bed, I knew what I liked, and Raven melted for me as if she had been waiting for this moment. Or maybe I was just wanting things that I knew were probably too much.

My balls tightened and I nearly came. I pulled out of her mouth and pulled her up to the couch.

"I need to find my fucking condom," I growled. I shucked off the rest of my clothes, got my condom out of my pocket, and slid it over my dick.

Raven's eyes were wide, but her hands were between her legs, touching herself, making herself even wetter, and I had to squeeze the base of my dick, trying not to come.

"Your nipples too?" she asked, eyes wide.

"You can tug on them if you want. With your teeth."

She grinned and reached for me, and when I kissed her again, positioning myself, we met each other's gazes.

"Are you ready?" I whispered.

"For you? Yes."

I didn't know exactly what that meant, and I couldn't think about it anymore. Instead I slid deep inside her, and we both groaned, her pussy hot and so fucking tight around my dick.

It took me a moment for me to fully pump into her, finding myself fully seated, both of us straining at the action.

"I need you to move. Sebastian. Move." She tugged on my nipple rings and I grinned, and then I moved.

Her nails dug into my back, deep enough to leave marks. I continued to kiss her, fucking her hard against the couch. The whole thing moved, and we bumped into the coffee table but it didn't matter. I just needed her, wanted her. I slid one of her legs up so it curved over my shoulder, and I fucked her harder, keeping her steady against the couch.

And when she came again, calling my name, digging those nails even deeper, I followed her, filling the condom, crushing my mouth to hers.

We were sweaty, slick, shaking. We sat there, trying to stay upright, and I looked down at her and smiled.

"Wow," I whispered. "I'm usually better at words than that. Sometimes."

She smiled up at me, her eyes dark, looking a little drugged and a whole lot fucked. "Wow's a good word. I don't think I've ever done anything like that. And I really want to do it again."

I smiled, knowing we could since I had all night. And I knew that was okay.

Chapter 10

Raven

"YOU'RE NOT GOING TO TELL ME HOW IT WAS?" GREER asked, and I closed my eyes.

"No. I'm not going to tell you. You don't need to know."

"I think we do," Daisy Knight said as she sat on my couch.

Daisy was one of Sebastian's many cousins and worked at the security branch on the other side of our building. Aria had brought her over when she and Greer decided to tackle me and force me into a partial girls' night. We all had early mornings, and things to do later, so it wasn't like we could do an actual girls' night of debauchery or whatever Greer wanted, but we could at least have a couple hours to have a glass of wine and apparently talk about boys.

"You know, I'm okay without the details. I think you guys are forgetting that Sebastian's my twin. Not just my brother, my twin. We shared a *womb*." She stretched out the word womb, and we all giggled.

"*Womb*," Daisy repeated, also stretching out the word.

I snorted, nearly choking on my wine as the two continued to say the word over and over.

"Wow, you guys are even weirder than I am," Greer said, shaking her head. "I love you both."

"You all are exhausting. That's what you are," I said with a laugh, as I reached down for a piece of cheese and a cracker.

"Which kind did you get?" Daisy asked, narrowing her eyes at me.

"Oh, the smoked Gouda. A good choice. The Havarti is my favorite, but the one I brought over has a little too much dill in it for my liking."

"You know, you're right," Aria said, biting into the Havarti. "It's good, because you can't go wrong with Havarti, but it does have a little too much dill."

Greer met my gaze, eyes wide. "I know we always joked that Montgomerys were addicted to cheese, but you guys just stopped a conversation about sex with hot men in order to talk about cheese. I think there needs to be like a program to help you through that or something."

Daisy and Aria laughed.

"Once again, he's my twin. I'm not going to talk about my brother's sex life."

"And you know he's kind of my cousin, though not by blood. So I don't really want to know too much."

"I don't understand how you guys are all so connected. Nor do I understand your fascination with cheese." I bit into the smoky Gouda again and sighed. "I mean, this cheese is fantastic. But it's not better than an orgasm."

"None of us said it was better than an orgasm," Aria said with a laugh, taking a bite of her cheese. "But I would miss both. And considering it's been so long since I've had an orgasm, I will take the cheese, and be a little jealous."

"Oh, dry patch? How long's it been?" Daisy asked, laughter in her voice.

"I don't want to talk about it. I'm pretty sure even my vibrator is about to leave me. It's been overworked."

We burst out laughing, and I shook my head. "You guys are ridiculous. I'm so glad that you're here."

"Okay, I guess we should not talk about cheese or sex, because it's getting Aria depressed," Greer said with a laugh.

"That is true. Not up to par cheese, and no sex

means I'm a sad person. A Montgomery with no cheese."

Daisy grinned. "You know what's funny, the love of cheese is not ingrained in our DNA. My mom is a Montgomery, but she didn't adopt me until I was older. It was just me and my dad for a bit. And yet, as soon as my dad married my mom, suddenly I'm in love with cheese. I think maybe it's part of their wedding vows and they sprinkled it onto me as the flower girl."

"I guess the more you have sex with Sebastian, the more you're going to want cheese," Greer said very solemnly, her eyes dancing.

"Didn't we just say we're not going to talk about either of those?" I asked, shaking my head.

"Okay well, on that note, I actually do need to go. I'm meeting with a new client tomorrow, and I don't want to deal with it."

Daisy winced. "Oh, I'm glad you picked the short straw on that one."

Aria narrowed her gaze at her cousin and coworker. "Just for that, you're sitting in on the call. I'm going to need backup." Daisy flipped her off. "You're not my boss. We're co-owners. And I'm technically older than you. So fuck no."

Daisy jumped out of her chair and ran as Aria chased her.

"Goodbye, we love you."

"You heathens," Greer said with a laugh. "Leaving

me alone with the woman who's freshly laid and making me jealous?"

Daisy slunk back in and picked up the plate of cheese. "If you're not going to eat this, we will."

"Take it. I really don't need it." I set my hand on my stomach, knowing I was actually going to regret eating so much soft cheese. With my illness, I shouldn't eat so much dairy.

"Are you okay?" Aria asked, as she came back in to help me clean up too.

"I'm fine. You guys can go since you said you had an early day."

"We can clean up after ourselves. We might chase each other around like we're Nora's age, but we can do this."

We cleaned up, and after all three hugged me and said their goodbyes, I closed the door behind them and rested my forehead against it. Everything hurt, and I hated myself for it.

I knew it wasn't my fault, I knew my body hated me, but it wasn't fair.

I slid into the kitchen, trying to take deep breaths, as I started the kettle to pour myself some tea. I'd relax, meditate, or maybe take a hot bath. Anything to get over the fact that I shouldn't have had cheese and wine in the same night, especially after a stressful week.

My doorbell rang. I frowned and looked down at the readout on my phone. Sebastian waved at the camera. I smiled, but also wasn't sure that I really wanted to let him in. He didn't need to see me like I was going to look in a moment. I switched off my electric tea kettle and dragged my feet towards the door, trying to at least fix my hair or something. With just the girls here, I hadn't minded that my hair was on top of my head and my face was devoid of makeup. But now I knew my skin was a little blotchy, a little clammy, and I wasn't looking well.

When I opened the door, he smiled at me, then took one look and frowned. "What's wrong?"

I winced. "I knew I looked bad, but I didn't realize I looked *that* bad."

He reached forward and cupped my face. "Your skin's clammy, baby. What's wrong?"

"I'm just not feeling well all of a sudden. It happens. I'll be fine, you can go home with Nora." I frowned and looked behind him. "Where is Nora? You didn't leave her at your house alone, did you?" I asked, alarm shooting through me.

Sebastian looked at me like I was an idiot. Well, I might be about some things.

"Seriously? I didn't leave my five-year-old alone at the house. Or maybe I did and she's learning to make ramen on the stove all by herself. She can almost reach it."

"Sebastian," I moaned, as I leaned my head against the doorway.

He cursed under his breath and, without saying a

word, picked me up and carried me inside. He closed and locked the door behind him, and I was too tired to do anything but just shove at his shoulder.

Whenever an episode came on like this so quickly, I knew it wasn't going to be good. I had to work tomorrow, I had a huge order coming in on top of the normal café work, so I needed to be on top of my game, and not be a damn idiot.

Girl time was needed, but I should have refrained at least somewhat.

"Talk to me."

"Where's Nora?" I asked again.

"She's with my parents. They have grandparent day. Mostly to show that there can be grandparents that aren't fucking assholes, and also because they love her. We lived with them for the first couple of years of her life, so she still has her own room and everything."

I smiled at that, pressing my hand to his chest. "I'm fine, just set me down. I was going to make some tea. Do you want some?"

He shook his head. "No thanks. But I'll make it. You go sit on the couch or something."

"I can take care of myself, Sebastian. I always have."

"And I come from a big family where we're forced to learn that we don't always have to take care of ourselves. Let me help you. Are you sick?"

"No. Not like that. If I was contagious or something I wouldn't have let you inside. I wouldn't want to get you sick, and I really wouldn't want to get Nora sick."

He smiled at me, something in his eyes that should worry me, but I ignored it. I had to.

"Look at you trying to take care of me."

"I'm fine."

"You're not."

At that moment my stomach rebelled. I rolled to my feet and ran towards my bathroom. I could hear Sebastian following me, and I ignored the embarrassment, the humiliation and fell to my knees, vomiting all the wine and cheese that I'd had that day. I didn't always throw up when an episode hit me, in fact, it was usually just fatigue, intense pain, or a random chin hair I wasn't used to. The weight gain and weight loss were normal.

I hated this. It wasn't going away. It was my life.

But it did change things.

And it wasn't like I could hide this from him.

Water ran behind me, and Sebastian put a cold washcloth to my forehead.

"Was it something you ate? Do you want me to call someone?"

He sat behind me, holding my hair as I heaved into the toilet, and I hated it. Everything felt gross, and I didn't know why he had to be so sweet just then.

"It's not something I ate," I said after a moment. I wiped my face on the towel, then my mouth, before I forced myself to sit up and out of his arms. When I pulled myself up, Sebastian steadied me. I brushed my teeth, used to this routine.

"Come on, let me tuck you in bed or something. Or get you that tea? What will help?"

I shrugged and turned, pressing my forehead to his chest. He was so hard, so strong. So I let myself lean into him. He wrapped his arms around me, pulling me close, and I wanted to cry. But I couldn't. Not right then.

"I have PCOS," I said after a moment, and Sebastian cursed under his breath. "You know what that means?" I asked.

He gently ran his hands over me, soothing me. And if the cramps weren't as bad as they were, I might have leaned on him more. "A couple of my cousins have it. It sucks." He winced. "Okay, that's a small word for it. It's a horrible thing that not many people talk about. What can I do for you?"

I had a feeling I was going to fall in love with the most perfect man. He hadn't acted weird, hadn't shied away. Instead, he knew what it was and wanted to make sure I had what I needed.

Damn him.

I shook my head, a little flabbergasted. "I just need to rest. I have a long day tomorrow, and if I didn't own the business, I could maybe take the day off, but I can't."

He winced but nodded before leading me to the bedroom. Without saying anything, he stripped me out of my clothes, and I narrowed my eyes at him.

"As much as I love seeing you naked, because I do, I'm not going to take advantage of you. Where are your pajamas?"

I laughed and pointed to the dresser. "I love how you ask that after you strip me so I'm only wearing my underwear and no bra."

"Sue me. I like your nipples."

I resisted the urge to cover them, but then he was pulling a soft tank over my shoulders, and then helped me slide into softer cotton pajama pants.

"Comfy?"

"Yes. Thank you." I slid into bed, and without another word, Sebastian took off his shoes and slid right in after me.

"Let me cuddle you. It's what I do. You're going to have to deal with it."

I snorted, but then cuddled with him. The pain came in waves, but then slowly subsided. I was just tired and throwing up had helped. Not the healthiest way, and I would add it to things I needed to talk with my doctor about next so I could see if there was something we could do. But it was life. There was something I needed to talk about with Sebastian though, something that was probably a little too early. But I was way too comfortable, way too tired to care.

And way too close to this man.

"So...you know all the symptoms of PCOS, right?"

He nodded against my head. "A lot of cysts, stomach

and back pain. Skin issues, hair issues, acne. You know, the fun things that we get in puberty."

I snorted and leaned against him again, feeling slightly better. "I have an IUD because I like to practice safe sex, and because it helps with the symptoms slightly. I was on hormonal birth control for a while, but it just made me feel weird. And I worked odd hours so I couldn't always take the pill at the same time. Things are different now, meds are different now, but this works best for me. I gain weight and I lose weight, and I have one cyst on my ovary that's so large at some point they're probably going to have to take it out."

I continued to talk about my symptoms, and with anyone else, I probably wouldn't have been this forward. But this was Sebastian. He had known me for what felt like nearly my entire life. He was the guy who had run to the store for Marley and me when we started our periods the same week. I'd had a single pad to take care of me during school, but Marley hadn't had anything. Her parents hadn't prepared her for it, so Sebastian went to get things for us because I couldn't leave her.

He grew up in a house of women, and a huge family that talked about their bodies and their health. It was such a foreign concept to me, but he had always been there.

We probably knew way too much about each other, and were still learning more, so he had to know this.

"Do you know about the other side effect?"

He sighed and nodded. "Yes. Though it's not a given."

I wanted to kiss him. He was trying to be so careful with me and I wasn't used to this. "My body doesn't make enough hormones to ovulate. And when that doesn't happen, my ovaries develop those cysts. It changes my menstrual cycle, it gives me all of those lovely side effects. And it also makes it really hard for me to get pregnant. I am in a support group online just to discuss different side effects and different treatment plans, and I know women with PCOS have children, but it was hard for them. I don't have all the side effects, but it's painful sometimes."

"My cousins talk about it, because they want to make sure the younger cousins who might not know about the condition understand it, but I'm sorry."

I was so jealous of his family. Mine was amazing, but we were a small unit of three. And they had a whole collection of family members who were there no matter what. "I don't know if I want kids ever, Sebastian. I'm not ready to think about that yet. And I know that you had to think about that far earlier than you wanted to. I love Nora, I always have since the moment I met her right after she was born and everything changed." I let out a breath. "Well, yeah, those are the things that go through my mind if I ever start a relationship with a man. Which, I know it's way too early, but I have to think about that. My future isn't set in stone, nobody's is. And we know that firsthand. But yes. There you go."

I hadn't meant to blurt all that, and it was probably ridiculous to even be having this conversation. But for some reason I needed him to know.

As I waited for him to respond, it felt as if my whole world were on a precipice. I waited to fall, I waited to see if he would catch me or if I would catch myself. Or maybe a little bit of both.

He leaned down and pushed my hair back from my face. "I'm sorry. I know all about choices and how sometimes we don't get them. So why don't you just rest right now, okay? I'll be here when you wake up."

I sighed and leaned into him, and had a feeling I had said a little too much. He wasn't leaving now, but he might. I had probably just ruined my chances with him. But things were a little too complicated as it was. So I would just go to sleep, and let him hold me.

And wonder if he would be there when I woke up in the morning. And if it should matter at all.

Chapter 11

Sebastian

"THAT'S ICING!" NORA SHOUTED AT THE TV, LITTLE fist in the air.

Ford snorted and rubbed his hand over his face. "A little bit. I think. I'm not good at figuring out icing."

Noah groaned. "You're my best friend. My roommate. How can you not figure that out? You should know it. We discuss it every time."

"Just like it takes forever for you to figure out what offsides is in football."

"Soccer. We're in America. You call it soccer." Kane, my cousin from the Colorado Springs branch of Montgomerys shook his head. His last name might be Carr, since his mom was the Montgomery, but he was still one of us. We didn't let go easily.

Noah sighed. "Both are legitimate terms for the sport. It's a geographical preference. One is not better than the other, but in a country where you use football interchangeably with two sports, you have to be careful. It's not like you go out and call it American football when you're talking about the Broncos."

"Please stop. For the love of God, please stop," Kingston, my cousin from Boulder said, rubbing his temples. "I joined this business with all of you so I could have a steady job and do what I like, but if we have to discuss sports terminology one more time I will scream."

"Don't scream, Uncle Kingston," Nora said, her eyes wide. "It's okay. I'll explain it to you." Nora climbed into his lap, her little Avalanche jersey looking adorable on her. My cousin just beamed.

"There we go. That's my best girl."

Leif just laughed, his body shaking as he looked at me. "I love the fact that she has been part of your guys' night since the beginning."

I shrugged, looking at my daughter as she explained hockey rules to Kingston as if Kingston hadn't played his entire life.

"Well, she was just an infant when we started. Teenagers watching hockey as my parents tried to not freak the fuck out that they were grandparents at a young age. It was fun."

"Well, I'm grateful you invite me."

"We're business partners, cousins, and best friends. Fuck off."

"Language," Nora called out, not looking at me but at the TV screen.

Leif snorted and handed me my beer. "Drink. You're fine."

"Why didn't you bring the boys?" Noah asked, digging into the pico de gallo with a tortilla chip.

"Put the pico de gallo on your plate with the spoon. Stop spreading your germs," Ford said with a grumble as he did it for Noah.

"They're like an old married couple," Leif mumbled, too low so that the others couldn't hear. Which was good, because Noah and Ford could kick our asses. While Leif and I were in the tattoo branch of the family business, Noah, Ford, Kane, and Kingston were all part of the security business. They were bodyguards trained in ass kicking, in tech and installing actual security systems, as well as setting security paths for high-tech companies. I wanted nothing to do with that. I might be big and inked, but I was frail in comparison.

"Anyway, the boys are with their mom tonight. Lake wanted to try the new recipe, so they're all hanging out."

"I guess Nora could've gone over with them, or even with Aria and everyone, but I like having her here for guys' night."

"It wouldn't be guys' night without her," Noah said,

this time tossing my daughter in the air towards Ford who caught her.

I rubbed my temple, my pulse slightly elevated. "Please stop doing that."

"What?" Ford asked, tossing a giggling Nora to Kane.

"We're having fun," Kane added with a tease.

He flipped Nora upside down, as she giggled, and then all of them were on the floor, play wrestling as Nora slid in between them, pretending to pin them down.

"You said that she was too small to toss her like a football before," Noah said very sagely. "She's bigger now."

"And you guys are still too rough," I said with a laugh.

"You say that as if you don't toss that girl in the pool at your mom and dad's house."

"But she can land easier," I said softly. "How the hell did I end up a girl dad, allowing this type of brutality in front of me?"

Nora giggled again before she threw her body on Kingston's back, and Kingston pretended to fall, until he was crawling around like a horse of some sort, and Nora proclaimed herself the victor.

"Okay, now I want a little girl. You think Brooke would want a third?" Leif asked, and Ford snorted.

"Please can I be there when you ask her? I'd like to be there."

"You're just asking for somebody to slap you upside the head, aren't you?" Noah asked, shaking his head.

"That's true," my cousin answered, smiling.

"I thought Tristan was coming?" Leif asked after a few moments, all of us focusing back on the game.

I shook my head. "Him and Taryn have a thing to do."

"They sure like fighting," Leif answered, understanding what code words I had just used.

"I think they like making up more," Noah said wisely. Nora frowned, her little lip poking out.

"What do you mean? When I make up with Molly and Shane, we all have to hug and say something that we like about each other. Is that what they do?"

I glared at my cousins, before I held out my hand and my daughter jumped on my lap. I held back a groan, since she hit a very important part of me, and was getting taller every day and would one day actually hurt me. "Yes. Just like that. Now, are you all fed? Do we have enough junk food in you?"

"Just a little junk food. You made me eat my vegetables before we came."

I laughed. "Because you're a big girl, and you need vegetables to stay healthy."

"Fine, I'll eat my cauliflower," Ford grumbled, and Nora clapped her hands. "Good. Daddy makes it the best."

"Does he now?" Noah asked, teasing, and Leif threw

a pillow at them, which got them all wrestling again, this time a little harder. I pulled Nora back and kissed the top of her head. "Let's watch the game. Their wrestling's a little too violent for you right now."

"It's okay. I won before so I'm the queen."

"Yeah, you are."

Nora bounced from cousin to cousin, explaining her day, and then watching the game with such interest that I knew that I'd have to get her in another pair of skates soon. She was a natural on the ice, even in her little baby outfit, and I didn't know if she wanted to add hockey to her sports regimen. There were a couple good peewee teams that she could grow into. But she was already doing soccer, dance, and art, and I didn't think I had it in me to do anything else.

"So, you and Raven?" Ford asked, and I glared at my cousin's best friend.

"No. Not doing it."

"You're not doing her?" Ford asked, his voice low.

I elbowed him in the gut. "Stop it."

"I'm just saying. You guys are hot together. I mean, if you hadn't seen her first and all..."

"Don't even go there, Ford."

"I won't. I don't stand in the way of a Montgomery and their prize. I know the rules." He sent a dark look towards Noah, and I wondered what that was about, but I didn't want to pry.

Because if I did, then they would want to pry into

what was between me and Raven, and I didn't have answers for them.

Nobody thought it weird that I was dating my friend from school, Marley's best friend. Nobody commented on it. The fact that they hadn't told me they were all thinking about it, and didn't want to rock the boat.

I didn't think they were judging, but they were worried I was going to feel something weird about it. And I might, but I didn't want to. So I was just going to suppress that feeling and not think about it at all.

The Avs scored and we cheered, Nora dancing in front of us. She and Kingston decided to do the dance they learned together when she was around two, which had way too much wiggling in it for their own good. I just laughed and sank back into the chair as Nora went to Ford, and they talked about who they thought was the MVP of the game.

I loved my kid. She was the best thing that had ever happened to me, coming out of the worst possible moment of my life.

Raven wasn't even sure she wanted kids. I got that. We lived in an age where society didn't force us to feel like we had to have kids to have a complete family. I had my Nora and I didn't know if I wanted more than that. But then again, we were still starting out. We weren't serious, Raven and I. The fact that Raven wasn't sure she would ever be able to carry a child? That hurt in the same way that I knew it hurt Raven. But it wasn't my place.

We weren't serious.

She had said she liked Nora. She loved Nora. So that was something.

I pulled out my phone.

Me: *You watching the game?*

Raven: *Go Avs! There's a lot of icing in this game.*

I laughed, and as everybody looked at me, I shrugged. They all knew who I was texting, and since Nora would be over to look over my shoulder at any minute, I made sure I kept it PG. Mostly because she was learning to read a little too well now. I'd have to be careful.

I'd have to be careful for many reasons.

Me: *What do you say to going to a game? The family has season tickets because there's so many of us, and we pitched in. I can get us a couple of seats this month, I think.*

Raven: *I've always wanted to go. I mean, I went I think once when your parents brought me and Marley. But I haven't been as an adult. So I can have beer while watching. Let's do it. Would Nora be coming?*

She asked about Nora right away, and that did things to me.

Me: *If it's not a school night. If it is, she'll stay with my sister or my parents. I don't want her to be out too late.*

Raven: *Okay, that works. And you're sure, Sebastian?*

I knew what that meant. Because she had opened up

a huge step for us. A huge moment that I could walk away from, but I wasn't going to. I wasn't that much of an asshole. I hadn't been that asshole when I was nineteen, and I sure as fuck wasn't now.

I didn't know what Raven and I had, or what we could have. But I wasn't going to walk away because there was a possibility she would never want or be able to have a kid. I wasn't that selfish.

Me: *Damn right. See you soon?*

Raven: *Of course. Give my love to Nora. And the guys.*

I smiled, set down my phone, and glared at Leif as I realized he had been reading over my shoulder. There really was no privacy in this family.

But the Avs scored again, and Nora threw herself in my arms.

I held my kid and felt that maybe this was okay.

Maybe we had something to look forward to.

Chapter 12

Raven

"Okay, you're right. Drinking an ice-cold beer while wrapped in a coat and scarf and watching men chase each other around with sticks really is the best way to enjoy your day."

Sebastian laughed next to me, a big hearty laugh that did things to me. It also sent a few interested gazes his way, and when I raised a brow at a woman leaning a little too close to him, she just winked at me. When she mouthed, "Good for you," to me, I beamed and settled in next to the big, tattooed man next to me.

I still couldn't quite believe I was here, with him. Because he hadn't gone away. He hadn't said this was too much.

I had never been so open about anything like that

before. I hadn't felt the need. There had been no one like him. And that was the problem, of course, but here we were, on an actual date. It was a school night so Nora wasn't with us. But she would've been welcome to join us.

Of course, I didn't know exactly how that would work, because then we would be here just as friends, wouldn't we?

"You have that little furrow between your brows. It makes me want to rub at it, but I don't want to bother your skin when you're getting so pink from the cold."

I turned to him and sighed. "I was just thinking that I'm sad that Nora's not here, but I'm also glad that we can just hang out. I don't know exactly what that says about me."

"She would've had a blast, she'd yell louder than any of us. Except for maybe my cousin, Kingston."

"It's too hard to remember all of you," I said with a laugh.

"You know him. He comes into your bakery more than I do."

"That's because I can go through the door and just bring you what I think you need for the day."

I smiled, a little warm at that thought. It had started out as a joke, us finally using the door between the two buildings so that way we could act like a big family. The door was behind the counter but in front of the kitchen so that way we were still up to code, but customers couldn't go through. The idea was just so our team members could. Greer and I had begun to bring coffee and pastries as well as sandwiches and other goodies over to them in the middle of the day, just because we could. And they helped out busing tables or serving food if we got too busy and they had a spare moment. It was oddly working out, and even Wyatt came over a couple of times to help. The security guys were usually out of the office, so I didn't see them as much. Their business tended to take them off the property. But I knew their coffee orders.

I especially knew Sebastian's.

"We're spoiled and I like it." He paused. "Why were you thinking about Nora being here?" he asked.

I winced. "Because I don't know how to act around her. I mean, I don't think I've changed, but does she know we're dating?" I paused. "I mean, if that's the word that we're using."

He was silent for a moment. Of course, there was an actual play going on, and the opposing team's goalie missed the puck and everyone jumped to their feet, screaming as the Avs were now up by one, but he ignored all that and hugged me tight and kissed me hard on the mouth.

"Dating's a good word. We're together. We're not with anyone else. We can use it. And no, I haven't brought anyone else around for Nora. But you've already been there."

"We're complicated," I whispered against his lips, but then remembered that others were around us, and this was a little too serious of a talk for an Avalanche game.

He tangled his fingers with mine, as we went back to watching the game, the puck moving so fast it was hard to keep up, players going on and off the ice as if they were in their own choreographed ballet. I watched the athletic trainer in front of us stare down the players, his finger touching each player's stick without even looking. Because as soon as their stick broke, they needed a new one, and he was there for them. It was brilliant, and if I focused on things like that, I wouldn't focus on the fact that he hadn't finished answering the question.

"I haven't sat down with Nora and talked about us. Mostly because everything seemed to be moving forward in a casual way. She knows that we're on a date. But I haven't asked her what she thinks. And I will. This dad thing is still pretty new to me, even five years in."

My heart raced and I squeezed his hand. Neither one of us was looking at each other because there was still a game on the ice, and we needed to beat Toronto. It was a rule in our house.

"I just don't want to say the wrong thing around her."

"You won't. You haven't. But yeah. I should probably talk to her. See how she's doing with this whole thing."

"Well, that won't be awkward at all," I said with a laugh, nervousness settling in.

"Thanks for that."

"Hey, one day she's going to be asking you for dating advice. Because she's going to bring a boy or a girl home that is pierced and tattooed just like you."

He scowled at me. "Really?"

"No, they're going to be an accountant. All strait-laced, slicked back hair, not a tattoo in sight."

"I'll have you know that we have accountants in our family."

"With no tattoos?"

"I didn't say that."

I snorted. The Avalanche won and we jumped to our feet, shouted, and he kissed me while others cheered around us.

"Ready to get out of here?"

"Yes."

"We can go to a bar, get a beer with a hundred other happy Avalanche fans."

"I'm good without a bar."

"Okay, then let's get you home."

A couple came up to us, with bright eyes and wicked grins.

"I was wondering if that was you."

"Hey, Leo."

"Hi, Leo. And you're May, right?" I asked, waving at the woman with short black hair and blunt bangs at

Leo's side. Leo worked with Sebastian, and May was the Montgomery childcare provider and organizer. The former nanny turned businesswoman was brilliant, and I had seen her come into the place a couple of times.

"It's nice to see you guys. Go Avs!" she said, putting her hands in a little spirit fingers position.

I snorted. "Are you a hockey fan?"

She looked around, eyes wide, and whispered, "I like basketball. Don't tell anyone."

"How could you?" Sebastian said with mock offense.

Leo just sighed. "I tried to get her to like football. But no, it's that. And tennis."

"I still have a crush on Rafael Nadal," May said, hand over her chest.

"You know, I was always a Federer girl, but yes, I swooned for Nadal."

We met each other's gazes and laughed, as the men at our sides just gave put-upon sighs.

"Come on, I need to get you home," Leo said, as he put his arm around May's waist.

"I don't mind. We can discuss sports ball all you want."

"You're killing me here," he said with a mock growl. They waved goodbye, and we each headed to our cars.

Sebastian turned up the music and we sang along to random indie rock and pop songs from our youth, and things just felt normal, as if we had always been here. Though we hadn't, and it was still new, but that sense of familiarity made whatever the hell we were doing now easier. We pulled into Sebastian's driveway, and I got out, rolling my shoulders back.

"That was fun."

"It was."

We stood in front of his car, and he reached his hands out. I looked down, confused, wondering exactly what would happen next. What *should* happen next.

"Come inside. Have a beer."

"But isn't Nora there?" I laughed. "Of course, Nora is there."

"She knows I was with you tonight. And I have family sleep over all the time."

"But no one in your bed."

"My brother slept in my bed once, because my sisters were in the guest room, and Nora didn't mind."

"I am not Gus."

"True."

He lowered his hand, but then moved forward, cupping my cheek. "Nora's sleeping. And you have baker's hours. She knows that I was with you tonight. We'll figure it out."

"If you're sure."

"I'm as sure as I'm going to be."

Not quite the answer I was hoping for, but then his lips were on mine.

I moaned into him, leaning close, when a wolf whistle sliced through the air.

"I have to get home and get to bed because I have an early morning. Go inside and stop giving the neighborhood a show," Noah said as he came forward.

I frowned. "I thought Aria was babysitting."

"Aria had to head out for a client, so Noah took over," Sebastian said with a sigh. "I'm lucky that Nora loves all of you."

"But I'm her favorite," Noah said. He walked over and kissed the top of my head.

I blinked, confused.

"Be nice to our boy. And have all the fun that I wish I was having." He saluted and walked away. I just shook my head.

"He's interesting."

"That's one word for it. Come on, Nora's in bed, but if she wakes up with a nightmare and realizes the house is empty, I'm going to have to kick Noah's ass."

I followed quickly, watching as Sebastian closed the door behind him.

Instead of getting a beer, or having a snack, or even having a chance to make things awkward, I slid my hand into his and we made our way down the hallway.

He checked in on Nora and closed the door quietly. I only caught a glimpse of Nora sleeping on her stomach, sprawled out like a starfish. Sebastian grinned and led me to his bedroom.

When I closed the door with a soft snick behind me, I let out a breath.

I hadn't been in his bedroom. We had always gone to my place, because Nora was here.

He cupped my face, gently sliding his fingers down my cheek.

"You're beautiful."

I laughed. "I'm sweaty from wearing a coat all night, and I'm in maroon. Nobody looks good in maroon."

"I'm not a liar. Don't fight with me."

"Are you sure, Sebastian?"

"I'm sure." And then his lips were on mine again and I sighed into him.

We had to be quiet. We gently stripped each other, and when I pressed him back to the bed, he grinned and I went to my knees.

I licked up his shaft, being careful around the piercing. The only person I'd ever given a blow job to with a piercing was him, but he was teaching me what he liked. And he was always a little rough, a little forceful. He slid to the back of my throat, gagging me, but I wanted it. His hold was tight in my hair, the moves a little rough, but it's what I wanted, what I needed. I scratched at the skin on his thighs, just as rough. We weren't soft and sensual. We were hard and fast, but as quiet as possible.

When he was nearly ready to come, he pulled out and tugged me up so I was straddling him. He sat on the edge of the bed, my legs straddling him, and lifted me by the waist.

I was already wet, but he used one hand to play with

me, and I put my hands on his shoulders for balance. He slid one finger deep inside of me and I groaned. Then he leaned forward, took one nipple into his mouth, and sucked. When he bit down, I shuddered, nearly coming just from that. I never came with breast play, but he knew what he was doing.

And then he was sliding me down onto his now condom-covered cock, his length stretching me to the brim. I was so full and he was nearly too damn big at this angle. His piercing hit that special spot inside of me, that bundle of nerves that always made me shake. My toes curled, and I moved so my feet were planted on the bed behind him. And then he lifted me up and down over his cock, slamming me onto him. Each thrust ached, to the point of pain but exactly what I wanted. My breasts bounced, both of us using our core muscles to fuck each other hard. The angle was too much, but not enough. I tugged on his shoulder and he smiled before tossing me on the bed. I rolled and we laughed, quietly. And then his mouth was on my pussy, his hands on my breasts. He plucked and tugged at my nipples as he ate me out, licking me and probing me. I came on his face, my legs wrapping around his neck. If he wasn't careful, I would suffocate him with my thighs.

I kept that thought to myself as he gripped me by my hips and flipped me on my hands and knees. Before I could even get out a shocked gasp, he plunged deep inside of me.

He pounded in and out of me. We shook, and I gripped the bedspread, pushing back on him. And when I came again, clamping around his cock, he followed, hovering over me, biting at my shoulder, whispering my name.

I clung to him, holding as tight as I could.

"I really hope we were quiet enough," he whispered against me.

I shook, holding back a laugh with his cock still deep inside me.

"If we're not careful, we could wake the neighbors. So let's be quiet."

He kissed where he had bitten and frowned. "You might have a mark there."

"You're going to have marks on your ass from earlier."

He laughed. "Serves me right. Let's get us cleaned up, and then I'm going to tuck you into bed."

I froze and looked up at him. "Are you sure? I can still go home."

We were quiet for so long I wasn't sure what he would say. What I wanted him to say.

Finally, he pushed my hair back from my face, rubbing his thumb over my lip. "Stay."

So I stayed.

Chapter 13

Sebastian

"Go, Nora!" I shouted, clapping my hands in front of me, as others in the stands cheered.

There weren't really stands, they were groups of parents in camping chairs, blankets, and others pacing around as they watched five- and six-year-olds kick a ball around.

I smiled as Nora kicked the ball, and shouted again because it was a damn good kick.

"She's a natural," Raven said.

I smiled down at her. "She is."

"And she's kicking butt. Although I have to say when

she invited me this morning, I wasn't quite sure what I expected."

I had been floored when after Raven had done a few things at the bakery that morning, she had come over to drop off a couple of things for us. I had ordered the snacks for the kids, so in addition to orange slices, the kids each had individual pastries, some gluten-free, some dairy-free, some sugar-free, because Raven wanted to make sure everyone could have something.

And when Nora had looked up at Raven and grinned, I hadn't realized that my little girl was about to change everything.

"Are you going to come to our game?" Nora had asked.

Raven had looked between us, eyes wide. "Oh. Well. I mean. I have your treats for you."

"But you're off work. Daddy said that you were bringing it after you were done working. So, do you have time? I want you to meet Molly and Shane. Please?"

Raven had swallowed hard again and looked at me. There hadn't been any other answer.

"Come on. You should come." I'd held out my hand, and Raven had looked down at it, before sliding hers into mine. Nora had clapped, and then she asked for a kiss from both of us, and then in the way that little girls were, had shouted for us to kiss each other.

"Please? Kiss, kiss, kiss!" she had called out, and because I listened to my daughter, I grinned, leaned down, and brushed my lips chastely against Raven's. "Good morning and thank you for the pastries."

Raven had looked at me wide-eyed, and honestly I'd felt a little flabbergasted too.

"Good morning. Well then…"

"Well then."

And that was how we found ourselves on the sidelines at a peewee soccer game, Raven shouting right alongside me.

"Greer keeps texting me that she's annoyed she's missing this."

I frowned. "Greer wants to come to a children's soccer game?"

"I think she wants to see *me* at a children's soccer game, but she likes things like this."

"Wait till we get to recitals. That's when we have to draw straws for which Montgomerys come to which."

"Do they all want to come?"

"We try to have at least four in the audience at all times. When I was younger there were enough kids that you could spread out the events. So if Aria and I had events at the same time, Mom and Dad couldn't go to both, but they could split up and send along an aunt or uncle or grandparent. We hadn't really cared in the end, because we knew that it wasn't them choosing one over the other, it was covering everyone's bases. We all took our turns, and it worked. I'm damn lucky that my family cares like that." I froze. "Tell me I did not just curse."

"You might have. But I don't think anyone heard." She paused. "Okay, probably everyone heard."

I shook my head, and then looked back to see Shane running alongside Nora. The two fist-bumped, and then continued to go against the other team.

"Those two are so cute."

"I think they're fricking adorable. Molly's the same way with them. They've all three just blended together."

I lifted my chin at Molly's parents and her mom waved at us, then Shane's parents did too. They were with their extended families today, as it was coming up on a holiday, so everybody was doing a thousand things at once.

"Well, I'm glad to be invited."

"It is hard to get a ticket in this place," Noah said as he came up on Raven's other side.

"Seriously. Since they don't want forty Montgomerys at an event, they sort of have to ration us."

I frowned at my cousin. "I thought Gus was coming today?"

"He had something pop up with a last-minute work thing. So I'm here. I hope that's okay."

"I'm glad that you're here," Raven said as she hugged him. Noah hugged her a little too tightly, and wiggled his brows over my head.

I narrowed my gaze at him, but I didn't curse or flip him off, remembering we were at a children's soccer game.

Nora dove on the ground, tripping over another kid. I nearly stepped forward, rage boiling through me, but Raven pulled me back and whistled.

"You okay, Nora?" she called out.

"I'm fine, Raven. Just got to get right back up, right, Daddy?" Nora called out.

I hated the fact that she had dirt on her knee and shin guards. No blood though, and she seemed to be moving all right, but I would check that knee later.

"She's fine, Daddy," Raven whispered.

"Don't call me Daddy. That really freaks me out," I said with a mock shudder.

She grinned. "Yeah, I can see that."

Raven looked past me, frowned, then looked between me and Noah before shrugging.

I looked behind me and noticed a group of the moms standing there, smiling widely in our direction while continuing their conversation. I looked back at Raven, confused.

"What was that?"

"Nothing," Raven whispered.

"Huh."

"Oh, Sebastian," one of the moms said as she came over.

I turned, nodded in hello. "Hi, Gretchen. How are you?"

"Oh, just enjoying the game as always. Is this one of

your cousins? We haven't met. We know all about you Montgomerys."

I cleared my throat. "No, this is Raven. She's a friend of mine and Nora's."

Gretchen looked Raven up and down before smiling. "It's nice to meet you. So, you're a friend then?"

And that's where it clicked, and I rightly called myself a fool.

Because bringing Raven to a function like this in front of all of the other parents was pretty much claiming her as my girlfriend. Or something that meant that she was part of Nora's life.

And gossip was always bad when it came to me. Because I was the former teenage father turned widower, but now I was bringing a woman to a soccer game.

I was never going to hear the end of it, and I was the idiot who dragged Raven in the middle of it.

"It's nice to meet you, Gretchen," Raven said, after I finished introducing her.

"It's nice to meet you, too."

She looked up at Noah.

"It's nice to see you here, Noah."

"Nice to see you too, Rachel. I mean Gretchen."

Noah had a mind like a steel trap, and he was just egging the other woman on, but as Gretchen's daughter was going to be in the same classes with Nora for a few more years, I shook my head at my cousin. No need for that kind of interference.

Noah shrugged, then went back to watching the game.

"So, what is it that you do, Raven? Do you have children too?"

Knowing what Raven went through, I knew that that question was insensitive as hell. And it wasn't something that I would truly have thought about, though I should have. Hell, I'd lost Marley in childbirth. I knew the complications of pregnancy, and Gretchen just threw that question out there without even thinking.

"No kids. I own a bakery and café. Latte on the Rocks? The new place."

"Oh. Next to Sebastian's tattoo shop. Interesting. I've been in there. The coffee's amazing."

"My best friend runs the coffee bar. Greer's amazing and fantastic at what she does. The best."

"So you're the baker then? I wish I could. We try to be healthy, you know."

I held back a growl, annoyed as fuck. I didn't know what this woman wanted, but I was done.

Raven just grinned. "I get it. I try to have a healthy mindset when it comes to baked goods. I don't need it as a treat, or as an excuse. I enjoy it. And I make sure that I have more nutritious options, and I don't shy away from sugar unless I'm forced to." She turned then, ignoring Gretchen, as she went to talk to Noah.

I raised a brow at Gretchen. "I'm going to watch Nora now. Good to see you, Gretchen. Now go tell all your little friends that I brought the woman that I'm dating here. I'm sure that's what they want to hear."

Gretchen went off in a huff, and I sighed. "I'm sorry."

"No, she just wanted to dig at me." Then she laughed, and I couldn't help but notice the beauty of her. There was just something about the way that Raven laughed. "Whenever someone finds out I am a baker, they either say I'm too skinny to be one, or I must eat all of my goods because I'm too fat. There are always those people that have an unhealthy relationship with the food that they eat because of what society, the media, and generational trauma brings them. I get it. But I'm trying to create something different. I love a healthy relationship with food, and I love baking. It brings me joy. So, I go on a rant sometimes and I'm sorry about that. However, she didn't come over here because I bake."

Noah whistled beneath his breath and hugged Raven hard. "I like you more and more every passing day." Noah laughed. "Seriously. Thank you for coming today. You've brought entertainment. Beyond the fact that my little niece over there is kicking butt."

I turned to Nora, who was on the sidelines waving at me. I waved back, as did Raven and Noah. "What are you talking about? Why did she come over here?"

Raven laughed and her eyes danced. "You're the *hot dad*. Even the non-single moms are hot for you. And some of the dads. It's okay. They wanted to see if there was a claim laid. And to get the lay of the land."

My cheeks heated. Noah turned away, but I saw his shoulders shake. "I'm exclusive. You know that. I've never slept with any of the moms here."

"That's fine. And I'm exclusive too. Nor have I slept with any of the moms. Or dads."

I snorted. "I've only had one girlfriend, Raven. I'm not good at this."

I hadn't meant to say that out loud, and I was grateful that I had said it low enough that I didn't think Noah heard.

Raven squeezed my hand before turning to watch Nora run back out on the field. "It's okay, Sebastian. I'll teach you how to be a boyfriend."

I felt as if a weight lifted off me. I didn't know why, but it felt damn good.

I just had to figure out what to do with this feeling.

Chapter 14

Raven

"You have pep in your step."

I turned to look over my shoulder at Greer and smiled. "Yesterday sucked. But I'm better today, and I am in the mood to make something different for lunch."

I was done with all my morning baking, and always left myself some free time on Fridays to either try something new, or to better a recipe I already had.

"I'm glad you're feeling better."

I smiled, then went to take out a fresh batch of rolls.

Yesterday had been a bad day, my cramps worse than usual. I had worked only half a day before I'd gone home—something I never did. I usually worked through the pain, but the problem with owning a business with your best friend meant that she made me put my health above our company's needs. So I had gone home and cuddled in bed. Sebastian had shown up not an hour after me, bringing me soup from my own bakery because he could, and then had made sure I was tucked in and comfortable. We had watched movies in bed while I worked on recipes in my notebook and he sketched. When he left me to go pick up Nora, they both joined me.

It felt like being a family, and it was just so different.

I didn't want to step into Marley's shoes, but then it hit me again and again that Marley had never had this opportunity.

I wasn't Marley. But Sebastian wasn't Marley's Sebastian. And maybe one day my brain would comprehend that.

We were slowly coming to terms with this new relationship of ours and finding a routine. And I was trying to lean into the fact that I was now dating a man that I had once had a crush on. It didn't quite seem real, but we were figuring that out.

"Earth to Raven. You're thinking about him again, aren't you?" she whispered as she worked on a mocha, and I began cutting bread for sandwiches.

"Maybe."

She gestured towards the open door between our two shops, and I shook my head. "Stop it. Not here." *Not ever.*

She rolled her eyes, and then went back to greeting customers. The shop had slowed over the past few weeks, but to a nice pace. We weren't overwhelmed like we had been the first couple of weeks, but we already had regulars, and new people were coming in daily.

I didn't want to tell myself that this was actually going to work, but it sure as hell felt like it.

The door opened and I looked up to see Wyatt coming in. He looked dejected. That was really the only word I could use that fit. He stood in line like he always did, waving and talking to others as they spoke to him, but he looked sad. And while I didn't know him as well as I knew the others in the building, I still wanted to make sure he was okay.

He ordered his coffee from Greer, who gave me a look and I nodded, working on his pastry.

"Here you go, Wyatt. How are you feeling?"

He shrugged, then took the coffee from Greer. "Thank you both. And not great. Cora dumped me."

My eyes widened. "Seriously? I'm so sorry."

"Yeah. I mean, I guess I should have expected it. She's amazing and sweet and wanted something else, I guess. Probably not a guy who just owns a bike shop. Who knows. It just didn't work out. I should stop pouting about it. If you guys can tell, I must look like I have a gray cloud above my head. It's time for me to drink some caffeine and get over it."

"I am sorry though." I reached out and squeezed his

hand. We were friends, and I was getting better at showing my emotions rather than hiding them.

He squeezed it back, smiling. "I'm okay. I'll find someone new, or I'll end up alone for a while. Dating might not be for me. You know?"

I nodded. "I know."

His brows raised. "But I thought you and Montgomery were dating. What do you mean you know?" I blushed and ignored the way that Greer wiggled her brows at me before going back to a customer.

"Well, I just know what it feels like to get dumped. Or to just not be in a relationship. But yeah, me and Sebastian are doing well."

"He's good for you. A good man. Baggage, but hell, we all have it. I wouldn't be here without the Montgomerys. They're some of the best people I know."

I smiled. "Same. Honestly."

Wyatt gave us a two-finger salute, and then headed out with his coffee and pastry.

I was nearing the end of my shift, since the shop wasn't open in the evening, when the hairs on the back of my neck stood up.

I turned to see someone that I really didn't want to see, but it wasn't like I could stop this. It was like a train wreck I needed to look away from, but I couldn't.

"Raven."

I looked directly at Marley's mother and swallowed hard. "Hello, Mrs. Erickson."

"We need to speak."

"I can spare you a few moments. I just need Greer to take care of this."

"No. You're going to talk to us now. It's about time we had this conversation."

I looked at Greer, whose eyes widened. "You can take time off now, or you don't have to. You do not have to."

Marley's mother moved forward. "I don't know who you are, but I don't need your interference. This is between me and this woman."

This woman. That's who I was now. After all this time, after so many years of me being their daughter's best friend, I was now *this woman.*

And I didn't need to deal with it. "Come on, let's go outside. We can talk there."

"So you can hide who you are? Don't you think your clientele needs to know they are supporting a home-wrecker?" Marley's mom spat.

We only had a few customers in the building, and they were our regulars. They looked between us but didn't step to interfere. If anything, they looked angry for me, but maybe I was just seeing what I needed to.

"Let's go. We need to speak outside. This is my place of business."

"Because you have a business. You think you are all grown up and have a right to come back?"

Come back? There was seriously something wrong

with this woman and the man standing behind her. This couple had always been hard on Marley and her friends, but they crossed more than a few lines since losing her. And while I missed Marley, I shouldn't have to deal with this. And I truly didn't need Sebastian to hear about this since he was going through so much with them already. "Really? This is my home."

"It wasn't your home when you left us," Marley's father said, his voice deep.

"I'm just trying to work."

"Yes, it must be nice. This is a nice place. You've done well." Marley's mother looked around the café that I had put my blood, sweat, and tears into—that felt like a home, that was a delight in my life—and sneered. Then she looked at me right in the face and lifted her chin. "We didn't even know you'd come back to Denver until I saw you at his home." She rolled her shoulders back. "You left her. You left Marley here with *him*."

Greer moved quickly, leaving through the door separating the two places. I didn't know why I felt abandoned by her, but she just *left* me to face this alone. The betrayal stung, but I lifted my chin and stared at the two people who had raised my best friend. My best friend who was no longer here.

"I went to college. Just like Marley and Sebastian did. I just happened to go out of state. I didn't leave her. We grew up."

Marley's mother growled. There was no other word

for it. "*You* grew up while my daughter died. Because of *him*. Were you always together? Did you cheat behind her back? Or is this a new thing? Tell me. How would my daughter feel to see that you have taken her place. Are you raising her daughter, too? What lies are you spewing to my grandchild?"

Staggered, I shook my head. "It was nothing like that. Sebastian and I were never together like that. They loved each other. And I wasn't here for any of what happened. I came back because this is my home. And you need to stop talking like this. It's not good for you and it's not good for Marley's memory."

"Don't you dare tell me what's good for my daughter. You were not good for her. You were always filth. Always different. And you brought him into her life and now she's dead because of both of you. You think you can just walk into this place and no one will notice? They're all talking about you. How you're sleeping with your best friend's fiancé. She would have hated you. And with good reason."

"Just stop," I said, my hands shaking. My customers were standing up, looking ready to come to my side, and I just wanted it to stop. I knew what they were saying was evil and it wasn't true, and yet it still twisted around all my own fears. I hated it. I wanted to scream and to fight back but that wasn't who I was. I wasn't good at confrontation, and no one had ever said things like this to me before. What was I supposed to do? I needed to be strong, because what they were saying were lies. And it was only going to hurt Nora and Sebastian in the end. Forget about me. I needed them to be okay.

"What you're saying are lies. You have twisted something that's precious without the facts. Maybe you're trying to heal, but I can't do this. You need to go. And if you don't go, I'll call someone to make that happen."

I knew the Montgomerys would help, they had a security business after all, but I needed them to leave without involving them. Because while what they said might hurt, the fact that part of it was true cut deep.

"You were always second best, and now you're trying to fill her shoes and you never will." And with that, they whirled on their heels and left, leaving me staggered, broken.

Greer came back into the room, eyes wide, with Noah behind her.

"Where did you go?" I asked, my voice shaking. I could not break. If I broke, this would be the end.

"I was trying to get help, but everybody was out. I'm sorry."

Noah came forward. "Are you okay?"

I didn't want Noah, I wanted Sebastian, but I knew that if he came, it would just be worse. Why did I want Sebastian to be there? I didn't need him. I just needed to be strong. I was a strong woman, and I could do this. I was not going to cry.

"I'm fine." I twisted my hands in front of myself and

let out a breath. "They just needed to vent, but they don't get to do that in my place of business." I turned to our last two customers and tried to smile, but I knew it was a little too brittle. "I'm sorry you had to witness that. I promise it will never happen again. How about a pastry on me?"

"Don't you worry about it. What they said wasn't true, and if they took one more step towards you, we would've ended it," the big man with muscles larger than my head said, his girlfriend nodding in agreement.

"I'm sorry about that, honey. You didn't do anything wrong. Are you okay? Do you want us to call someone for you?"

"There's no need." We turned to see Sebastian standing in the doorway between the two businesses, storm clouds in his eyes, his arms folded over his chest. "Greer called."

I turned to my best friend, eyes wide. "Greer!"

"What?" she asked, chin raised. "He needed to know."

"This is my business. I'm sorry about all of this. To all of you. I handled it. Maybe not right away like I should have since I was trying to give them the benefit of the doubt. But it's my business."

Sebastian stomped towards me and kissed me intensely, a kiss that nearly made me melt before I remembered why he was here. "No. It's *my* business."

And then he left so abruptly that it took me a moment to realize what had just happened.

"Fuck." I turned to Noah. "He can't go after them. If he does something, they'll arrest him."

"Shit," Noah said, pulling out his phone.

"No. I've got this. It's about time I handle this." And then I tossed my apron on the counter, picked up my purse, and followed the man that was going to break my heart.

Chapter 15

Sebastian

I KNEW IT WAS BAD. I KNEW THAT THERE WERE SOME things that were never going to change and there were going to be things that made me want to scream. But I hadn't realized it had gone this far. I should have, with the way they talked to me and from the way they made my daughter feel. It didn't matter how many times I talked to them and tried to be polite, they didn't listen. Fuck that. Fuck being polite. I was done.

I stormed towards my car, ignoring my cousin calling out to me.

"I've got this," a familiar voice said. Noah mumbled

something to her, but I ignored them. I could not deal with this right now.

"Sebastian! Where are you going?"

I turned to see Raven running after me, bag in hand. I couldn't have her here and think. I was so damn mad and yet I wanted to wrap Raven up and keep her safe. "Go back to work. I have things to do."

"Whoa. No. I won't just leave when you're standing there looking as if you want to hit something. You can't leave when you're this angry over something that you can't control."

"Raven. I just need you to go inside. I can handle this." I tried to take a breath, but my chest was tight and I needed to scream or do something other than stand here in the parking lot.

And then she was in front of me, cupping my face. I hated that. Because I just wanted to lean into her, but I couldn't. I needed to feel righteous in this anger because if I didn't I would back away and then Marley's parents would keep hurting the people I cared about. This was the final straw. Or perhaps it had been the final straw too long ago and now I was done fighting my anger.

"What's your plan here?"

"I'm going to do what I should have done a long time ago—confront them."

She shook her head, and I narrowed my eyes.

"If you do that, they'll get their lawyers. You know they will."

I winced and took a step back. The lack of contact burned, but I needed to pace. Nobody was paying attention to us in the parking lot, and I was grateful that people were going about their day, but all I wanted to do was scream, to fight something, fight *someone*.

"They told my daughter that she killed Marley. And when I confronted them that time, and every other time, I've been calm, I've been rational, and nothing's come of it. They've gaslit me, they've lied to me. And they're hurting their granddaughter."

"And then they came in here. I get it. But I'm fine. I can handle this. I have always been able to handle them."

There was something in her tone, something I didn't understand, and it worried me, because I didn't know what she felt about me, what she felt about this relationship. Everything had moved so fast, it felt as if we were living a completely different life than we had even a month ago. But I needed to put my daughter first, and that meant I needed to deal with whatever the hell Marley's parents were doing.

"What she said was terrible. What they've always done is terrible. But you going in there angry isn't going to help. That's what they do. That won't solve anything."

"I should just stand back and let them hurt my daughter? Hurt you?"

"Of course not. But you chasing after them isn't going to help."

"How do we know that? I haven't tried it yet." I slid my hands through my hair and paced some more. "When Marley died, they tried to take her away from me. You know that, right? I had to fight for custody of my own daughter because they thought I couldn't handle it. And the thing is? I was nineteen. I was nineteen fucking years old. I didn't have a college degree, I had part ownership of a business that Marley's parents hated. And on paper I looked like shit. I was just some tattooed boy who wanted to do more tattoos, who hadn't finished college, and had gotten his girlfriend pregnant."

"You're more than that, you know that."

"Maybe? At the time though I was lost. I was fucking drowning, Raven. I didn't even have time to mourn Marley. I was too busy trying to figure out how to change diapers. I thought I knew how. We went to all the classes, but when Nora was kicking her little feet and screaming and scrunching up her little face and getting so red and angry, I didn't know what to do. My parents saved me. Aria saved me. My cousins saved me. We joke that my family is so big that we could take over the world, but they took over my world. I wouldn't have made it without them."

"And you've got them now, too. You don't have to do this alone."

"That's the problem. I have never been able to do anything on my own. I had to live with my parents for the first couple of years of Nora's life so I could save money to live on my own. Marley and I thought we could do it on our own, in our own little apartment. And we would've struggled but we would've found a way with the two of us. But the ghost of me couldn't have done it without my family. And Marley's parents used that against me. They took me to court to try to take full custody. And when that didn't work, they tried to take half custody. And they chipped at me day by day until they got the two weekends a month. They take my daughter away from me and I have to deal with whatever they say to her when she comes back and she hates it. I know she wants to love her grandparents just as much as she loves my parents. But it's different, and I'm done. They're twisting the narrative. They're hurting my daughter, and they're hurting you."

"They're hurting you, too. I can handle it."

Again, there was a lie in that tone but I didn't know where it came from.

"I need to talk to them. Because they don't get to do this. I'll try to be rational. but I don't know if rational has ever worked."

"Then we'll go together. Because it isn't just your family here to help, I am, too."

I shook my head, but then she put her hands on my chest, just a gentle caress, and I wanted to scream.

"I don't know what to do."

"You're doing just fine. You've got this. I'll go with you. I'll stand by your side, and you can talk to them.

Because what they did was not right. I could have had them arrested for trespassing or something. Maybe I should have, if that would've helped you."

I shook my head and pressed my forehead against hers. She calmed me, and I didn't know what that said about us.

"No. Because that would hurt Nora. And that's the problem. Because Nora loves her grandparents. And they're a part of Marley. My daughter doesn't have her mother anymore. She never did. Marley never got to hold Nora. And I will hate that until the end of my days." I swallowed a lump in my throat, hating that I felt like I was going to cry. I didn't cry over Marley anymore. I mourned, I grieved, because you never stopped grieving, but it was different now. And yet talking about Nora's grief, the lack of her mother in her life and everything we had done to try to fill that void, made me want to break down.

"You have done an amazing job as her father. Your parents and your siblings and cousins have all stepped in. I even watch you around Leif's children, and you're an amazing Uncle Sebastian. You pay that back. You are all there for each other and I love it. It's how a family should be."

"There's something wrong with Marley's mom. Marley's dad might just let her walk all over him now, but there's something wrong with her. I don't know how she twisted into this. They've always been a little hateful towards me. And way too judgmental."

Raven nodded. "They hated me too. Because I wasn't perfect."

"None of us were. We were the three musketeers."

"I'm sorry. I'm sorry that she's gone. I miss her too, Sebastian. And I hate that I wasn't here for it. I hate that I left."

This was something else we needed to deal with, but I ran my hands through my hair. "We already went through this, didn't we? You left because of school and I apologized for being an asshole."

"You weren't an asshole. Okay, maybe you were. But we were kids, we're allowed to be. It was a very complicated time then."

"When I confronted you at my house? Or when you left?" I asked, trying to bring some levity to the situation even though I didn't feel it at all.

"Come on, let's go talk with Marley's parents."

"You sure you want to go with me? That's putting you right in the line of fire."

"Maybe. But you don't need to do this alone. You might think you have to because you don't want to lean on anybody but the problem with that is you have a wonderful family. So if it's not me, it's going to be Noah or it's going to be Leif or someone. You have an endless number of family members who want to take care of you."

I pushed her hair back from her face and did what I should have done when I saw her stand up to Marley's parents, pale and shaky, yet not backing down. I leaned down and pressed my lips to hers. The kiss started off gentle, just a bare brush of lips, before it deepened just enough to show her that I needed her, that I wanted her.

I didn't know what we had between us, didn't know if this was right or if we were making a mistake. But I kissed her because I wanted to. Because I just fucking needed to.

She sighed into me, I kissed her one more time before I moved back.

"Let's go. Let's get this over with."

She slid her hand into mine and squeezed. "Okay. You've got this. *We've* got this."

I wanted to believe her, but I had a feeling this was only going to get worse.

By the time we made it to Marley's parents' house, it had been over an hour since the incident at the café. But their car was in the driveway, so at least they seemed to have come straight home.

"Are you ready for this?"

"As ready as I'll ever be," I murmured. We got out of the car, and I wondered if they were going to call the cops on me. I wouldn't put it past them.

Raven pulled her hair back, wiping flour from her chin I hadn't even noticed.

"You look great."

"I look like I've been working all day."

I looked down at myself. "Same. Maybe if we were dressed in suits and looked like bankers this would go better."

"If we looked like bankers, then I wouldn't even recognize us."

I snorted, then the reality of our situation hit me when Marley's father opened the door and glared at us.

"You can just leave. I'm not having this."

"No, Mr. Erickson. You're going to want to let us speak, or I'll be talking to my lawyers."

There. That sounded rational and reasonable. And not like I wanted to throw up.

"Are you threatening me, son?"

"No, I'm not. I'm also not your son. We both know that, and I think it's about time we had this discussion. Because us going around it and snapping at each other just isn't working."

"Let him in. I have a few things to say," Mrs. Erickson said from behind him, her voice breaking with anger.

I fisted my hands at my side, stiffening. Raven sucked in a breath, and I wanted to reach out. But touching Raven right now would put their attention on her and not on me. And I needed them to pay attention to me.

Marley's dad stood back, glaring at us, and I realized that it didn't matter what I did with Raven in that moment, they'd hate us both anyway. But I wasn't going to shun her, wasn't to push her back just to make the Ericksons more comfortable. So I reached out and took her hand.

Raven's eyes widened, as if she was surprised I was claiming her in front of anyone. But fuck that. We were together, and we would deal with this. She was standing by my side for this. I wasn't going to pretend she was just my friend.

The gesture wasn't lost on the Ericksons, who narrowed their gazes.

We walked inside the modest ranch home with its three bedrooms, a long hallway filled with pictures of Marley, and now Nora. It looked pretty much the same as it had when we were growing up. I hadn't been allowed here often, because they hadn't wanted Marley to be with a boy, but I had been here enough.

I knew why they hated me, at least part of it, and I blamed myself for the same reasons, but there was no bringing her back, so this needed to happen. For Nora, for Raven, for my family, and for me.

"I can't believe you'd just show up here. And you brought *her*."

I squeezed Raven's hand before I let go because I needed to keep my head clear so I could think. Raven nodded at me and stood by my side. No one offered to get us a drink, for us to have a seat. We stood there, glaring, not a word spoken so I decided to break the silence first.

"We need to talk. Because what happened today can never happen again."

"Really? You're going to come into our house and tell us what we can and can't do?" Mr. Erickson asked, his voice low.

"I'm not saying what you can't do in your own home, but in our places of business, and what you say to my daughter—I do have a say in those."

"We loved her," Marley's mom said, her voice breaking. And then she was standing right in front of me, hands shaking. "And you killed her. You killed my baby. You, with your sins. You just had to get what you wanted, you defiled her. You got her pregnant and you weren't even married. My daughter had a full life in front of her and you killed her. I won't let you ruin my daughter's child. Just like you ruined my daughter."

She had said something similar before, but not with such hatred and hurt in her voice.

And each word cut, a slice to the chest, to the gut, to the soul. She was saying the same things I had thought to myself year after year.

Marley and I had loved each other. We had sex. And when she got pregnant, we decided to keep the baby and define our next phase in life.

And then a medical alert and a very unlikely pregnancy complication happened.

I couldn't take that back.

"No." I said after a moment, needing to breathe. I

shook my head, then looked at Raven, who gave me a tight nod. I saw the pain in her eyes, knew she hated this for me. But we would deal with this. "We're not doing this. I loved Marley. And I wish every day that Nora could know her mother. But that's not going to happen." I let out a deep breath and met their gazes. We needed to talk about this. We needed to stop accusing and I didn't know what to do, so I just said what had been bothering me since Nora was born.

"I can't regret what happened with getting Marley pregnant though," I said, and they looked as if I'd slapped them. "I can't, because then I wouldn't have Nora in my life. Do you understand that? When you conflate the two, you put that sin and that terror and that pain that you feel on my daughter. And I can't let you continue to do that."

Mrs. Erickson looked as if I'd slapped her. She put her hand over her chest, her eyes wide. "That's not what I mean. I love Nora."

"Do you? Or do you just want your daughter back? Because I sure as hell do."

I felt Raven start beside me, but I had to finish. I had to make sure she understood what I meant. "I loved Marley, but she's gone. And I've spent the last five years dealing with that. We made a choice to continue the pregnancy and became parents. And fate had other ideas, and she was taken from us. I will regret to the end of my days that you don't have your daughter. But Nora doesn't have her *mother*."

"*I know.* I know she doesn't have her mother."

"And you said that Nora killed her mother."

Mrs. Erickson's eyes widened, her hand going to her chest. "I never used those words. We talked about how Marley was gone and looking down on us from heaven. We were talking about her mother and writing notes to her so we could remember her. But I *never* used those words."

I wasn't sure if I believed her, but she did love Nora. I was just so afraid that the way that their love was twisted was hurting my daughter, and we needed to fix this. "Finding a way to live in this world without Marley nearly killed me but I didn't get a choice. I didn't get to wallow in my grief because I had a newborn who needed me and she was stuck with only me. We're trying to navigate this life without Marley." I paused, trying to think about what I should say without making this awkward. I just hoped to hell I wasn't doing it wrong. "And Raven? She has brought so much joy to us. So much light." I could feel Raven's eyes on me, her mouth open trying to say something, but I shook my head. "You can't threaten that. You can't put your hatred of me onto her. Raven has done nothing to you other than love your granddaughter. And I will fight in the courts again to keep you away from Nora if you are going to put so much hate into my daughter's life. She doesn't deserve this." I paused, my heart racing. "Marley's memory doesn't deserve this. Think about what you want your daughter's legacy to be. Will it be your hatred, or Nora's happiness?"

We were silent after that. I saw tears streaking down Raven's cheeks, and I slid my hand into hers, squeezing, as I looked at Marley's father, who stood straight-backed, pale-faced, lips pressed tight, staring straight at me.

But it was Mrs. Erickson that broke the silence when she started crying, shaking her head. "Don't take her away. I don't know what's wrong. I don't know what's wrong with me. I'm sorry. I hear the words and I know they're wrong. I just want my baby back."

"Marley can't come back. But Nora is *here*. Get help and stop fighting me. Because I can't do this anymore—I won't. I won't let you hurt my daughter. So fix it. Find a way to heal, because the words coming out of your mouth? That's not what Marley would've wanted."

"I'll try. I'm sorry."

The words floored me because she had never apologized to me before. But maybe this was the breaking point, because I wasn't even sure Marley's mother recognized herself. She shook her head and broke down, a keening wail ripping from her throat.

I wasn't sure that I had ever heard her break down like that. She cried in the hospital and at the funeral, but I didn't know if in these five years she had let herself feel anything but hatred. Because it was easier to hate, than to feel the pain.

Mr. Erickson held his wife close and nodded at me.

I didn't know if this fixed anything, I didn't know if it would, but I pulled Raven away, and we left without saying another word.

Because there wasn't much else left to say.

I just hoped that maybe, just maybe, this time what we'd said would work.

Chapter 16

Raven

"I AM NOT WEARING THE TENTACLES."

Greer blinked at me, her dark eyeshadow intention-
ally a little manic, her red lipstick smeared, and she was
still working on getting her hair to look like she'd
touched an electrical socket.

"You know, I didn't realize that would be a sentence
I'd ever hear from you."

"I'm not doing it. I'm going to knock into
everything."

"The tentacles are like an extra skirt. They tie off
and tuck in and you can take them off after the photo."

"I should have just gone as Sarah Bailey. That would've been better."

"Sarah to my Nancy Downs. That's the only way."

Greer winked and went back to fixing her hair. She was going as Nancy, Fairuza Balk's character from *The Craft*. It was one of our favorite old movies, and we watched it once a year around this time.

We had played "Light as a Feather, Stiff as a Board" and other games in college just for fun, but we had never dressed up as the characters.

"Are you sure people are going to know who you are? I mean, you don't have the others in your circle."

"Nancy didn't need the others in the end, did she?" she asked, doing the character's laugh.

"You were just in love with Skeet Ulrich the whole time, weren't you?"

"Always and forever. You can't stop me." Greer went back to working on her schoolgirl skirt. I held back a snort, working on my purple makeup.

"I'm glad that we found this top so I wouldn't have to paint my arms or anything, but my entire face is purple. I'm very confused why I said yes to this."

"Because that little girl asked you to be Ursula to her Ariel."

"Isn't that sort of like the evil lady compared to the princess? Is this something that I need to worry about? Is it like a subtle hint that she hates me and wants to spear me with a very large trident or something? Or didn't she get like stabbed by the ship? I don't remember."

"First, spoiler warning about *The Little Mermaid*."

"That movie came out before we were born," I growled.

"True, but still. Second, Ursula is cool now. She was just misunderstood. Ariel signed a contract."

"And Ursula tried to get Ariel out of the contract, and she used the eel, my second favorite henchman, by the way, in order to get Ariel to lose."

"The fact that you have a second favorite henchman just tells me that you're perfect for this role." Greer paused. "The first favorite henchmen are those from Hercules, right?"

"Seriously, I should have just gone as Meg."

"Meg would've been awesome. You can go next year as her and sing her song with that bluesy voice you can do. Would you want Sebastian to go as Hercules?" she teased.

"Honestly, Hades was hotter," I said with a snort.

Greer tossed her head back, laughing hysterically. "That is the best thing I've ever heard. And true. And then Nora could have gone as what, the goat?"

Giggling, I should my head. "He wasn't a goat."

"Fine, she could have gone as the Pegasus."

Imagining Nora with little wings, headbutting everyone around her, made me smile. "It doesn't matter. She asked me to go as Ursula, so I am. And she's Ariel, and Sebastian is Triton, and I'm kind of worried about what I'm going to see."

"You really want to see him in a fin, don't you?" Greer asked, teasing.

"I don't want to talk about it." Mostly because I had no idea how to answer that.

"Well, I can't wait to see everyone's costume. This is my first Montgomery party."

"It's not my first, but it is my first since I moved back. And my first since dating a Montgomery."

"You're in a relationship."

I crossed my fingers in front of her face. "Don't say things like that. It's bad luck."

"How is saying that you're in a relationship while you're *in a relationship* bad luck?"

"I don't know. Seriously, the tentacles are going to run into everything."

"This is why they're more like a skirt, versus all out there ready to knock down things. You'll be fine. And you can play with Sebastian's tail all night long."

"Why are you making this dirty?"

"Because I read too much tentacle porn," Greer said with a laugh as I followed her out, doing my best not to wiggle my tentacles around.

"More things I never would've thought we would say."

"Ursula and Triton weren't even a couple; this is a

very weird costume. I feel like I'm just going as the evil menace."

"First, you're not the evil stepmother, so there's that. Second, you know Ursula and Triton would've been a good couple. They're hot as fuck. All curvy and muscley and he has that daddy vibe going and she taught all about body language."

"This is a Disney movie you're ruining for me."

"You got drunk right along with me when we had daddy issues about King Triton. They would've made a good couple." Greer paused. "Minus the whole killing people thing."

I laughed so hard I nearly tripped over my own tentacles and made my way outside to Sebastian's place.

This was his first time hosting a big party for his family and friends apparently, and because he was a Montgomery, they were going all out.

His grandparents—the couple who had had eight children, who now mostly each had children of their own—would be taking the kids away for a great-grandparent night at their place, but many of the Montgomerys who weren't working and could come, were going to be there. People had other parties and events to go to, but this was a big one.

There were countless cars I didn't know in my driveway since I had offered it up, as had a couple of neighbors who had also been invited. That way the street did not look like it had been attacked by Montgomerys. Plus, many people had taken ride shares and carpooled so they could drink safely. They had this down to a science.

Kids' laughter filled my ears as I moved, and some of the neighbor kids ran around, smiling. Greer did her best crazy smile at them, straight from the movie, and they giggled before running away.

"Oh good, I'm scaring children. I have the old witch on the corner thing down."

"Well, you tried. You already got the old part down."

I tried to run away from Greer, but again nearly tripped over my tentacles. That's when I looked up to see green scale-covered leather pants, a gold belt, and a very muscular and tattooed chest.

I practically swallowed my tongue, looking up at Sebastian who had a fake white beard and white hair, complete with gold crown, holding a trident.

"Oh my God," I whispered.

"You're like if Aquaman and Triton had a baby, a very sexy baby," Greer whispered from my side. Sebastian just rolled his eyes.

"I had a shirt, one with fake muscles on it. Then my cousins and sister stole it, and so here I am."

I looked down at his nipple rings, then up at his face. "Are those nipple rings starfish shaped?"

"They were a gift from Leif. Let's just not talk about it."

He leaned forward and kissed me. I groaned but

held back from moving forward. "This purple paint isn't supposed to rub off that easily, but let's not try it out."

"Oh, we're going to try it out later. Just to see."

I blushed under my purple paint and Greer clapped her hands. "Oh gosh, I'm sorry I'm going to miss that, but I really don't need to watch you have sex. Okay, let's get inside, this witch needs a drink." Greer danced her way inside and met with the other Montgomerys. Some dressed as the Addams Family, some as horror characters. Some from an anime that I vaguely knew. There was even a whole *Avatar the Last Airbender* section of the Montgomerys, and that was the group I wanted to be part of.

"Is your neighbor dressed as Zuko?" I asked, eyes wide.

"Stop staring at him like that."

"I don't know. Zuko's the hottest cartoon character ever. And the fact that your neighbor's girlfriend is dressed as Katara? Perfection."

"Really, you are a Zuko and Katara fan?"

"Just in fandoms, not for the show. A girl can dream though." I fluttered my eyelashes, and he laughed, looking me up and down.

"You're a very sexy Ursula. You can't help it."

"You're here!" Nora called out as she ran to me, flinging her arms around me. I wobbled on my tentacles, and Sebastian steadied me.

"What did I say about tackling the fish in this household?" Sebastian asked, his eyes dancing.

I glared at him, then looked down at the most perfect little Ariel I'd ever seen. She had on a skirt with a tail on it, and a top that was made to look like skin with a purple clamshell tank top in place of the bra from the cartoon.

"You're adorable."

"I know right?" she said with a grin. And then she turned, and I threw my head back and laughed.

Hand-drawn all over the back were fake tattoos. All of the characters from *The Little Mermaid*.

"Daddy drew them."

She whirled to face me again and smiled. "Thank you. For being Ursula. I know she's the bad guy, but I still love her. She sings the best."

Nora was seriously the cutest kid ever. "Really? I'm just so glad that you invited me to be part of this."

"Of course. Because you're Daddy's best friend. Just like me." She flung her arms around us, and I blinked back tears, wondering how I could be part of this. But it felt right. I ignored the curious stares of some of the moms from Nora's school. They had to wonder, but I didn't have the answer myself. Though I did hold back a growl as they looked Sebastian's shirtless body up and down. No thank you.

Nora pulled us through the rest of the family, and we waved and laughed, making our way to the photo booth.

Nora slipped her arms around our waists, standing between us, so we knelt down for the picture. I looked over at Sebastian, wondering how this had happened.

He didn't ask me to step away, didn't want this to just be his and Nora's time.

I was part of it.

And it scared me so freaking much.

Pictures taken, cake eaten, the kids were dragged off to Grandma and Grandpa's, but they were laughing and dancing all the way, so it looked like they were happy to be dragged away.

Then the music got a bit louder, everyone started dancing, and Jell-O shots might have been involved.

We were having a little too much fun, and my tentacle skirt was now off, hidden in Sebastian's closet for safekeeping. Sebastian had his arm around my waist, my butt pressed against his very hard cock, and I was doing my best to hide him from the rest of the party.

"You're a menace," he whispered against me.

He had lost his beard along the way, as well as his wig, but someone had put the crown back on him, so he just looked like a younger Triton, all inked up and sexy as hell.

"You're the menace."

"Get a room!" Noah called out, drinking and dancing with a few other friends.

My head was a little dizzy, but everything felt good. I would probably regret this in the morning, mostly because I'd had way too much alcohol and dairy, but I would deal with it. It was worth it. Tonight was worth it.

The music changed to something slower and everyone booed, so Sebastian pulled me out through the kitchen to the backyard.

"I'm not having sex with you in a bush," I blurted.

Sebastian pressed his face to my neck, his entire body shaking as he pulled me towards my backyard. "There's a gate here, I'm taking you home, and I'm going to have my way with you."

"You're leaving your own house and your own party?" I asked.

"It's a Montgomery party. They'll take care of it. And I already nodded to Noah and Kane, so they know what's up."

I stopped dead on my feet, blinking at him. "You told your cousins in some hidden language that you're taking me away so we can go have sex in my house?"

"That was that chin nod."

"You mean a chin nod explained all of that?" Was I too tipsy for this conversation? I didn't think so, but maybe I would never understand men and their chin nods.

"Yes. Now come on, I want to see how far down that purple goes."

"Oh no you don't."

"Oh yes I do." And then Sebastian flung me up over his shoulder, carrying me fireman-style to my backyard.

Somebody saw us and cheered, but then everyone went back to their own lives, partying and having way too much fun.

Thankfully my keys were in my bra and he got us inside, and pressed me against the door.

"You have purple paint on your chin," I said with a laugh.

"You know what? I don't mind being covered in purple. But let's not get it all over your house."

Sebastian dragged me to my shower, and we were laughing as we stripped off pieces of costume along the way. He stuck the crown on my head, but pulled on my dress. I wiggled out of it, tossing off my shoes and panties. The dress had a built-in bra, so Sebastian's eyes went dark when he saw my naked breasts, reaching out with his hands to cup them.

"So fucking hot."

And then his hands were lower, between my legs, but I pushed him towards the shower, afraid to get purple paint from my face and neck anywhere else.

He turned the shower on full blast and, before he could say anything, I went to my knees.

"Holy fuck. A purple dick? That's going to be fun to wash off later."

"I'll keep you clean," I said, before I swallowed him whole, humming along him. He wrapped his hands in my hair, pulling tight, as he began to slide in and out of my mouth. I swallowed, letting the tip of his dick reach the back of my throat, and did my best to relax, letting him go deeper. He was rougher this time, but it was what I wanted. My pussy was already so wet I knew I would be drenched by the time he filled me. He kept going, the gagging sounds filling the shower, and when he was nearly ready to go, he pulled out and pulled me up. It was a slight burn, a slight pain, but it was exactly what I needed. He kissed me, hands on my breasts, in between my legs. He pumped two fingers in and out of me in quick succession. I nearly came just then, one leg up, trying not to fall. He pressed me against the shower, and kept fucking me with his fingers, his gaze on mine. It was just like that, a quick brush of a thumb along my clit, and I was coming.

I kept kissing him, leaving smears of purple paint all over him and it didn't matter. We were covered in it, and water and everything else. Suddenly he left me cold in the shower. I blinked at him, before he ran back in, condom in hand.

I groaned, helped him tear off the wrapper and wrap it over his dick. He was so thick, hot, and ready. He lifted me, and I wondered how he could do that in one swift motion. But his muscles didn't strain, he was all strength and sexiness. The sight of his tattoos nearly sent me over the edge. His cock filled me in one quick thrust that burned and ached and felt as if he were stretching me, and I came again, shaking. It didn't make any sense, I wasn't normally like this. And yet, with him I was. I pulled on his nipple rings and he groaned, pumping in harder and faster. We kept kissing, my fingernails drawing down his back. I knew I would leave marks, and not just from purple paint. I wrapped both legs around his waist, keeping us steady as he fucked me, pumping into me so hard that I knew that this was the first and the last and everything.

I wanted him. I needed him.

I loved him.

I loved Sebastian Montgomery.

And when we came together, I wrapped my arms around him, laughing and smiling and looking at him. He smiled back, looking as if he had not a care in the world. As if the world wouldn't change with those thoughts in my head.

So I didn't say them. I didn't say anything.

I just kissed him, and let tonight be about tonight. I knew tomorrow would come too quickly.

But tonight we had this moment.

Chapter 17

Sebastian

"AND THEN MOLLY SAID THAT BECAUSE I AM NOW THE sweeper, I should make sure that I have my cala sten."

I frowned, paused in the action of packing her school lunch for the next morning and blinked. "Calisthenics?" I asked, trying to come up with the word that Nora was trying to say.

"Yes. That."

My lips twitched and I tried not to smile. I didn't like my daughter feeling as if I were making fun of her, but that was a different word for her. "Molly used that word?"

"Sort of. She tried at least. And then her mom

corrected her, but I still don't think it's right."

I was oddly relieved that I wasn't alone on that precipice of parenting and confusion.

"I think I need to run more."

"You already ride your bike next to me when I run. And you have dance, and soccer practice, and I know you play on the field at recess. Your calisthenics are taken care of. But I can talk to your coach if you want to make sure that you add more? Though I don't think you need to."

Nora was five. I was honestly a little surprised she'd even tried to say calisthenics.

"Okay. I like the cupcakes that Raven brought." Nora beamed up at me, her face covered in chocolate.

I sighed, my lips twitching into a smile as I got a paper towel, wet it down, and began to wipe the chocolate off my daughter's face. "I can see that. Though it looks as if you got more chocolate on your face than in your mouth."

"Oh, I ate some. Thank you for letting me have a cupcake."

"You're always allowed to have a cupcake when I have them. It's very lucky that we have Raven, who bakes. Because I'm not great at making them."

"You're still my favorite. And you make good brownies."

I grinned. "I do make good brownies."

"But Raven's are better."

Once again, put directly in my place. But that's what my daughter did. She was too cute for her own good. "Okay then. Raven is the best. She's a baker, that's what she does."

"I want to learn to bake. Do you think Raven will help me?"

I went back to finishing up Nora's lunch for the next day. "I think so. You can ask." I paused. "Or I can ask for you."

"No, I'll ask. I know she's busy. Just like you. But I want to make sure. And Greer? I love her."

"She's great."

"But I'm too young for coffee she said. She did say that she could help me with foam art. What is foam art?"

I explained, laughing as she asked me question after question about Raven's bakery.

The two of them had clicked right away. I liked that she had connected with Raven as if they had always been in each other's lives.

"The holiday pageant is coming up too. And they're telling us who we're going to be soon."

I nodded, going through what I needed for dinner the next day to make sure I actually had meat out. Meal planning and making sure that I actually had things for Nora was really the only way I got through the week.

"What are the options?" I asked, half distracted.

"It's going to be all holiday themed, so I might be a star."

I looked up, grinning. "You're already a star, munchkin."

"You keep calling me munchkin, but I think I like it now."

"I try."

"Daddy?" Nora asked, her voice a little tentative.

I paused what I was doing and looked over at my daughter.

"What is it, Nora?"

Nora had her head bent, her little teeth biting into her lip, the napkin crumpled on her plate.

"What is it?" I asked again, coming around the island so I could stand right in front of her. I tilted her head up and pushed her hair back. "You can talk to me about anything."

"Do you love Raven?" she asked, her eyes wide.

My heart stopped. I hadn't expected the question, but I should have. Raven and I had been dating for weeks now, had gone to a party as a couple, as a goddamn family with Nora. We still went on runs together, she had dinner at my house. She even slept at my place some nights, though we were careful so Nora never saw Raven in her pajamas or anything. We didn't want Nora to feel awkward, and yet here I was feeling awkward when she looked scared to even ask the question. Maybe scared wasn't the right word. Nervous?

I didn't know why, but suddenly my mouth was dry and I couldn't quite catch my breath.

I wasn't sure what I was supposed to say, what words were good for this. But I needed to answer. Because my daughter was brave enough to ask, so I would be brave enough to answer. Even though I didn't have a good reply. I hadn't let myself think too far ahead. Because if I did, then things would get real.

Only they were far past real now.

"I don't know, Nora." I paused. "She's special to me."

Nora played with her fingers, sighing. "Mommy was her friend. Right?"

I swallowed hard, my pulse racing. "They were best friends. Just like I was best friends with both of them. Mommy loved her very much."

"If Mommy loved her, that means Raven must be amazing. Right?"

I tried to follow the logic but nodded. "Raven is amazing. She's the best."

Then my daughter looked up at me, her eyes wide. "Is she going to be my mommy?"

The world fell from beneath my feet, and I tried to keep up, to scramble for any handhold. "What?"

"When Tommy's dad married his new wife, she became Tommy's mommy. Is Raven going to be my mommy?"

I blinked and said the only thing I could in that moment. "No. She's not your mommy."

It wasn't quite the answer, but what was I supposed

to say? Raven and I hadn't even discussed anything beyond what we were doing. I needed time, we needed time. There was no easy answer for this.

"I love her. Is that okay? That I love Raven. I don't know what to call her, but I love her because she's Raven. And I think she loves me."

I swallowed the deep knot of tension in my throat and nodded tightly. Then I hugged my daughter close and kissed the top of her head. "She's the best."

"I know."

"And I know she loves you too."

"Okay. I like her a lot. And I would be okay if she was my mommy. Because she was friends with my real mommy. So then I'd have two."

At that, she hopped off her stool. "I'm going to go get ready for bed. I love you, Daddy."

Feeling as if I had lost my concept of reality, I nodded. "Okay. Brush your teeth."

"Okay."

"I'll be in to tuck you in, and make sure you're all set."

"Okay. I love you, Daddy."

And then she left, and I looked down at my hands, wondering what the hell I was supposed to do now.

A noise caught my attention, and I looked up to see Raven standing in the doorway from the living room, a box in hand. Her face was bone white, her mouth parted.

"The back door was open. You should lock that. I just brought over the cookies for Nora's class, like you asked."

I blinked, only now remembering that she had said she would come over with the cookies that she had offered to bake for Nora's class party, and I had left the back door open so she could walk right in. Because we hadn't exchanged keys yet.

"Oh. Thank you."

She set the box down on the island, then looked past me down the hallway.

"I heard. I'm confusing her."

"No, I think I am," I said, running my hands through my hair.

She stared at me, eyes wide. "I didn't mean to do this. To hurt her."

"You're not hurting her." I began to pace, trying to focus. "I don't know what the fuck I want, Raven." I hadn't meant to say that out loud, and when she took a step back, I felt like I had slapped her.

"Okay then. Good to know I'm not a replacement, Sebastian. I've never been. If you don't want me, fine. But I'm not a replacement."

Her eyes widened, as if she hadn't meant to say that, but she had, and now I had to deal with it.

"You're not a replacement. You're Raven."

"And I'm not Marley."

"I sure as hell know that," I grumbled. But I didn't

mean it the way she took it, and I knew that, but I couldn't take those words back.

"I don't know what I'm supposed to do. I didn't expect this. I didn't expect to come here, to come home, and find you again."

"What did you expect?" I asked, my voice cold.

"I expected maybe to find my friends again. But I didn't expect to fall in love with a little girl. To want to be in her life." She paused, looking at me. "To be in your life."

"You're right, we are confusing her."

She flinched, and I needed to say something. To say that I was the one doing this. That I needed to be the one that set boundaries, or to take them down. But I couldn't. Because I hadn't expected this, I wasn't ready for this conversation, but here we were. I needed to not fuck this up.

"Nora is amazing. And yours." I looked up at Raven's words, at the tears in her eyes. "She's yours, Sebastian. And Marley's. And I can't be Marley." Her voice cracked at that, and I took a step forward. Stopped. "No one can be Marley."

Marley was gone. But I wasn't that Sebastian, Marley's Sebastian, anymore. Somehow, I was becoming Raven's Sebastian. And I didn't know what that meant. Because it wasn't just me. It was Nora, too. I needed to figure out what I felt, and how it affected Nora. But Raven was standing here right now, and I wasn't saying the right things.

"I know no one can be Marley. I'm going to do what I should have done in the first place."

My head shot up and panic seized me. "What?"

"I should go, before things get more complicated. Before I hurt that little girl in there. I should go. And you need to just think."

"Just like that. You're just leaving?"

"It's for the best. I don't want to hurt Nora."

A single tear fell, and I wanted to reach out, brush it away. But maybe this was for the best. Everything had gotten too complicated too quickly. "Then go. Because I can't deal with losing anyone else. Or confusing her."

She paled impossibly further and nodded tightly. "Fine. I'll see you around. Like always. Tell Nora that the cookies are for her class."

She left, and I didn't follow her. I couldn't. Because if I went after her, then I would have to say something. And I didn't know what.

Did I love her? Would I allow myself?

I loved Marley and she was gone.

And I had broken when it happened, and Nora was left without her mother. I didn't want to do that again. I couldn't. And yet I hated myself. Because I didn't have answers. And I was past needing them.

Now Raven was gone, and I knew I had just made one of the worst mistakes of my life.

Chapter 18

Raven

MY BODY ACHED, AND I KNEW IT WAS MY OWN FAULT. I had been up the entire night before, due to the stress that had sent me into whatever type of reaction I was dealing with.

I had a rash on my chest, and I felt like if I moved too quickly I was just going to want to collapse in a pile and forget the past two days had ever happened. But I couldn't do that. PCOS was no joke, but I'd dealt with it for years and I would deal with it now. I still had to close up shop for the night and make sure that we were ready for the next day. I didn't normally close and then open the next day, but I was taking Greer's shift because she was dealing with a few things, and then needed to go on a trip to find help for another vendor.

I didn't mind working this many hours because it meant I would have fewer hours at home, fewer hours to dwell on the fact that I was in love with my neighbor, who had let me just walk out.

Perhaps I shouldn't have left the way I had, but what other choice did I have?

He hadn't wanted me to stay. He didn't love me. He didn't want me in his life for more. It wasn't fair to Nora, nor was it fair to me for it to continue.

I did not want to be Marley's replacement. I couldn't be. But I had accidentally thrown myself into that situation and the only way to get out of it was to cut ties.

I let out a snort as I cleaned up the final table in the room.

There were not going to be any cut ties, not when I worked and lived next door to the man. His family owned the building I worked in. His family friend owned my company. His family owned my house.

We had been complicated and tied up with each other well before we slept together. Well before I had fallen in love with him.

I'd had him in my heart for as long as I could remember, but I had ignored that pull to him years ago. Why couldn't I have continued to do so?

Why did I have to be that person?

I hated myself. Hated how it felt as if I were making mistake after mistake.

I hadn't spoken to him since I left, and he hadn't reached out to me.

Greer knew, of course. Because there was no hiding bloodshot eyes and a red nose.

And that meant the rest of the Montgomerys would know soon, because Greer would want to fix things. But I couldn't let her. I couldn't do this anymore.

Everything hurt—my body, my soul, everything. I wanted this pain to be over. But I knew I couldn't just sleep through it. I had to deal with the consequences of my own actions.

My fingers slid up to the necklace that I hadn't worn in weeks. Marley's necklace. The one that we had shared.

I stood alone in my café, the front door closed but not locked yet because we were still open. But the door between the tattoo shop and us was locked. On my side, and maybe on theirs too.

I looked toward the ceiling, like I could see the sky above me. "I don't know what to do, Marley. I feel like all I do is make mistakes. I left because I needed to grow up. I needed to be me without the two of you. And I hate myself for that. It was so selfish. I didn't want to only be your best friend. I didn't want to be the third wheel, even though you never made me feel like one. I didn't love him then." I let out a breath, my voice shaky.

"He was yours. I know that. I would never have loved him then. But I love him now, even though I think he's still yours, Marley. And I don't think it's fair to any of us, especially your daughter, for me to continue. I love Nora, Marley. I love her so much, but she's not mine. She's yours. And it's not fair that you're not here. You should be here."

I wiped away tears and then went back to my broom, to finish sweeping up for the day.

I was so tired. I just wanted to find a resolution but I knew it wouldn't come. "It's weird that I rarely talk to you anymore. Maybe it was because I felt as if I was encroaching. And it turns out I was. He was always waiting for you, never for me. I didn't realize that until it was too late."

"You're wrong, you know."

I whirled, broom in hand, as a scream tore from my throat.

Noah held up both hands, eyes wide. "Holy fuck. I'm sorry. I didn't mean to scare you. I thought you saw me come in."

"As I was just having a conversation with myself, one that was very private, I obviously didn't."

"Oh shit, I'm sorry. Seriously. I'm sorry."

"No, it's okay. I'm just going to go crawl into a corner and hide for a bit, and maybe go change my underwear because I think I just peed myself."

Noah snorted. "Well, I think I just did too because oh my God you scream loudly."

There was a bang on the door, and then my phone buzzed.

"I startled her, she's fine!" Noah called through the door. They banged again, and Noah pulled out his phone. "Let me text Leif right now. If we're not careful, the entire Montgomery Security team's going to run over to try to save you."

"I'm fine, though I'm going to lock the front door."

"You should. You're closed up now."

"I wasn't five minutes ago. I got distracted."

"Lock the door behind me after I leave, but I'm telling the guys this now. Actually, I'm telling the security group chat as well, that way they don't rush over here. Because you know they will."

I cringed, wiping away tears. "They don't need to. I'm good on my own."

And with that, I burst out crying. Noah looked panicked for a minute before he came up to me and cupped my face. "Stop crying."

"Because you don't like crying?"

"That could be part of it. But because he's not worth crying about."

I sniffed and wiped my tears on his shoulder. "That's not a very nice thing to say about your cousin."

"I don't have very charitable things to say about him right now."

"Is that a convoluted way of saying you know he dumped me?" I asked, my voice breaking.

"Greer mentioned that the two of you are no longer seeing each other. But she was very sparse on the details. I guess I'm going to have to kick his ass."

"Don't," I whispered. "I think I'm the one who dumped him. Though I'm not quite sure how it happened. I just realized that he's never going to love me. And I didn't want it to seem like I was trying to take Marley's place."

I didn't know why I was telling Noah this. I hadn't even told Greer everything. But for some reason, I could not bottle it up anymore.

"You know, for a man who is a brilliant father and a brilliant artist, he's not very good with the whole communication thing. He's never really been good about it, you know."

"He was okay at it."

"He was okay at it with Marley. And you. But he hid a lot of himself, because things got serious really fast with Marley. You can't get someone pregnant in college when you're both technically teenagers, and not go through serious crap."

"I wasn't here for all of that."

"Well, let's just say things went a little haywire. I mean, the family was supportive. Marley's weren't, of course."

I rolled my eyes. "Understatement of the year."

"Truth. But he hid himself. He was so worried trying to do the right thing for everyone else, he sort of forgot to freak the fuck out. I think Leif finally got through to him a little, because he can't really hide things from our eldest cousin."

"Well, he was pretty clear that he didn't want me. He doesn't love me. He said so."

The pain cut, but I did my best to ignore it. If I dwelled on it, I wasn't going to make it out of this in a semblance of wholeness.

"Damn it," Noah grumbled. "I see the way he looks at you. The way he treats you. There's *something* there."

"Something that could end up hurting Nora." I huffed. "And myself. But I don't want to confuse that little girl, and I don't want to be Marley. Maybe I'm a horrible person to think that."

"I'm sorry."

"Me too. I'll be okay. And Nora will be okay because she has your huge family. And since I live next door and work next door, it's not like I can really get away from it, you know? It'll always be there. No matter what I do."

Noah winced. "Shit."

"Pretty much. I will deal with it later. I just need to breathe. Things moved too quickly."

Noah raised a brow. "Or maybe not quick enough." He leaned down and kissed my nose. It surprised me, and I looked up at him.

"What's that for?"

"You're our friend. You're going to have to deal with us. And I don't like seeing any of my friends hurt. It's going to be okay, you know."

"Really?"

"It will be. You both want the same things, I think. I don't think you're listening to each other."

"I would say that's a rather astute observation, but you couldn't be more wrong."

"You know I suck at my own life. I really have no idea what I'm doing there, but with others? I'm okay."

"Whatever you have to say to help yourself sleep at night. Now, I'm going to clean up, and then go home and take a bath and forget. I think that sounds like a good idea."

"You're going to have to deal with this one day. Both of you are."

"Maybe. Or maybe Nora will grow up with a wonderful family, and I'll be that friend who's always there making cupcakes. Nothing more."

"But nothing less," he whispered before he left. I stood there, broom in hand.

I needed to fix this. To not feel like this. Only I didn't know how to change it.

The door opened again and I looked up, ready to say that we were closed, when Wyatt walked in.

"Hey, I heard about you and Sebastian."

I sighed and rubbed my hand over my heart. "It's

okay. I guess I know how you feel now. I'm still so sorry about you and Cora."

Wyatt smiled as he came closer. "Me too, but don't worry, Raven. You'll be seeing her soon."

I frowned, wondering what in the world he could mean, when his fist came at my face, and then there was nothing.

Chapter 19

Sebastian

"YOU ARE AN IDIOT."

I looked up to see Noah glaring at me from the doorway.

There were clients with Tristan and Taryn, but the rest of us were cleaning up, getting ready to end our day.

"I don't have time for this."

"Fuck off," Noah spat.

I blinked, surprised at the vehemence in his tone. "Excuse me?"

"You heard what I said. Fuck off."

"Oh, this is going to be nice," Nick said as he sat back, hands over his stomach.

Leo laughed. "Let me know how it goes, I'm headed out to go see my wife. But seriously, I want to know."

I saw Leo salute us from the corner of my eye, but I just stood there, staring at Noah. "Did you just tell me to fuck off?"

"Pretty much. Because you are so in over your head, you don't see what's perfect for you."

I pinched the bridge of my nose, exhausted. "I'm going to need you to start at the beginning. And stop cussing at me."

"You broke that girl's heart over there, and I want to know why. Why you think what you did is okay?"

"Hell," Nick muttered under his breath.

The rest of the crew settled in to watch, including the clients currently getting tattoos.

"I don't see how whatever's happening between me and Raven is any of your business."

"You see, that's where you're wrong. Because whatever's happening between you and Raven? Once you finally figure out what the hell you want, maybe you'll stop hurting each other. And as we care for both of you, you need to figure this the fuck out."

Nick snorted. "This is good. I should be taking notes."

I flipped Nick off. "Again, none of your business."

"It is, though, because I really like Raven. I like her for you, and how she fits in with the rest of us. So I don't understand why you two just can't talk it out and get over yourselves."

"What happened?" Leif asked, and I realized that everyone was staring at me. Lake came out from the office and sat next to Nick, arms folded over her chest. My cousin just raised a brow at me, and it was hard to hide my feelings.

But they had always known everything about me. The people in this room were the first people I'd ever told that Marley was pregnant. And they had held me up, with glue and tacks and tape when Marley died.

"Nora asked me if Raven was going to be her new mommy."

Everyone winced, and Lake came forward and cupped my cheek. "I'm sorry. That had to be tough for you. But she was so brave for even asking, don't you think?"

"Nora isn't the problem." I cursed, and moved away so I could pace. "Or maybe that's exactly the problem. She's only five. And yet she was brave enough to actually ask when I've been doing my best not to think about it at all."

"Do you know what you want?" Leif asked.

"I don't know. Maybe? I liked how things were going."

"You mean up in the air with no idea of what a future looked like, and possibly hurting everybody all at once?" Noah asked, and I flipped him off.

"It was working."

"Working so well that your daughter wanted answers that you didn't have, and in the end you hurt everybody."

"She left me."

"Did you ask her to stay?"

"I didn't have time to ask her to stay. She said she didn't want to hurt anyone and promptly left."

"Probably because she was confused and hurting, just like you. You guys need to actually talk. To communicate. To say what you want."

"Well, what do I want?"

"You're the one that needs to answer that," Nick put in.

"I don't know. I like having her in my life. I love the way she is around Nora and all of you. It just seems like she fits. But then I remember the fact that we've been friends forever, and Marley was always there, and then it gets weird."

"It could just be that you guys are finding your own way around this. Nothing's going to be easy. It never has been. You lost Marley way too young." Lake smiled softly at me. "But you don't have to live in that pain. You were healing. You were smiling and laughing. It doesn't hurt her memory to do that. Especially with someone that she loved too. Marley would be happy for you." Lake winced. "And I hate being that person telling you what someone else would've felt. But it's the truth, and you know it. Maybe that's what scares you."

I threw my hands up in the air, aware that everyone was staring at me.

"I don't know what to do."

"Get over yourself," Nick and Leif said at the same time. They stared at one another and snorted.

"I'm sorry. That's sort of what you told us to do back when we were fucking up with our women," Leif answered.

Lake nodded. "And I do thank all of you for helping Nick and me figure out what we wanted."

"Losing Marley was the worst moment of my life combined with the best moment. And I don't want to feel that way again."

"You have done so much, you're doing so much. Pain is always going to come at us and we're not going to know when it will hit us, but we have to feel that joy. And the thing is, you're feeling like shit right now without her. So why not take a chance on happiness?"

I looked at my family, my friends, and cursed. "I'm an idiot."

"There you go," Noah put in. "Go over. Talk to her. She's cleaning up and then going home. I can go pick up the munchkin if you want."

Lake waved us off. "No, I'll do it, and then have some auntie time. You guys go fix your love lives."

"I'll go with the love of my life so we can practice this whole family thing." Nick wiggled his brows, and Lake laughed. I just stared at my family, wondering how I could be this lucky, and how I could fuck things up so quickly.

"Go. I'll finish cleaning up your area," Leif put in.

"And I'm going to go back to my office. I have paperwork to go through," Noah said, as he saluted me and we headed out.

The door between the shop and the café was locked, and I knew that was on me, so I went to the front door, and what I saw had my blood freezing in my veins.

"Noah!" I screamed as I opened the door, knees shaking.

"What?" Noah asked, boots stomping. There was more shouting as Ford and a few others followed.

I stared at the ground, at the blood on the tile, at the knocked over table and chairs.

"What the fuck just happened?"

"She was just here. She was fine," Noah cursed.

"Fuck. Do we have the tapes? Do we have the footage from security?" Nick asked, and Ford whipped up the tablet in his hand and began to search.

"Pulling it up now. Call the cops."

"On it," Noah whispered.

"What the hell?" I asked, moving forward.

"Don't touch anything."

I waved off Noah, needing to do something.

"Raven! Raven!"

But there was no answer, just blood on the floor and nobody here.

"What the fuck happened? You were just here."

Noah looked at me with wide eyes, phone to his ear. Ford turned to the screen.

"It was Wyatt. Wyatt took her."

I stood there, confused as hell, worried that I was too late.

Again.

Chapter 20

Raven

COLD SPREAD ALONG MY CHEEK AND I TRIED TO OPEN MY eyes, only my eyelids felt so heavy. Where was I? Had I fallen asleep at work? No, that didn't seem right. It didn't feel like my bed, either. I couldn't be sleeping at Sebastian's.

Not anymore.

That familiar pain settled in, but this time it was mingled with a different one. An aching one, and I swallowed and tried to remember.

Noah had left, and I tried to close up. But then someone else had come in. But who? Why?

My face ached, as did my side. Something felt sticky

underneath me, and when I finally was able to lift my eyelids just a little, the bright overhead lights nearly blinded me. I shut them again and let out a pained moan.

"Good. You're awake."

Then everything came back to me all at once.

Wyatt. Sweet and adorable Wyatt. The man who ran the bike shop next door—had hit me.

But that didn't make any sense. Maybe I was just imagining it. Maybe I was just putting a familiar face on a monster. A nightmare.

But no, that also didn't make any sense. How could this be happening?

My arms ached, and I realized I was lying on the ground, wherever I was, but my arms were still somehow above my head. My shoulder felt as if it had been yanked, and my cheek ached, and everything burned. I wanted to throw up, but I had to figure out exactly what was going on.

Eventually, I was able to open my eyes, and see what I had missed.

What we had all missed.

Wyatt sat on a wooden chair in front of me, his eyes filled with sadness, his hands clutched in front of him. He looked so normal. His dark blond curls were pulled back from his face, as if he had run his hands through his hair enough that he'd styled it that way. He had on an old T-shirt with his favorite band logo, jeans with a hole in the knee, and skater shoes. He looked like he always did. He always wore casual clothes, unless he was in his spandex bike attire.

He sold mountain bikes and racing bikes and bikes for children. For the everyday biker and those who wanted to try a triathlon.

And he had hit me.

I slowly sat up, my body aching as I tried to figure out where I was. Maybe a basement?

Why would I be in a basement?

The floor was cement, cold, and my chains, actual *chains*, were loose enough that I had been able to rest my head on the floor while unconscious. Now that I was sitting up, the chains were above my head, allowing my shoulders to relax slightly.

I turned, trying to see everything that was in here. But there were just a couple of chairs and some old boxes marked with clothes and other random miscellaneous attire. But there was something else, something I didn't want to see. There was a woman. No, that couldn't be right. But there she was, with her hands in the same position as mine. But she wasn't moving, she had to be passed out.

I tried to see if her chest was moving, if she was breathing at all, but I couldn't.

When I realized who it was, I screamed.

I screamed as everything hit me, and the reality of my situation came forward.

I was chained in a fucking basement with Wyatt's ex-girlfriend. I didn't know if she was dead, or if she was just unconscious. This had to be a nightmare. A goddamn nightmare.

"Stop it!" Wyatt called out. "Don't make me hit you again. I really don't want to hit you. I just needed to get you here and I didn't know how else to do it. It's not like I own a taser or anything."

I stopped screaming and swallowed hard, staring at the man whom I'd thought was so nice, so kind. So normal.

But he was none of those things.

"Wyatt? What's going on?"

"You're fine. Cora's fine. She's just sleeping. She screamed at first, but then she stopped. But she's just fine. I make sure she's fed and watered and taken care of. I make sure she's happy. Because she wasn't happy before, but now she is. Because I love her. Just like I love you, Raven."

I didn't want to think about what he meant. I couldn't. I didn't want to think about what was going to happen next. I needed to get out of here. It didn't make any sense.

"Why am I here? I don't get it."

"I was really sad when Sebastian got to you first. But then you said you had a past with him. And so I maybe understood. And I had Cora. She's so nice. But she's not you. But she's trying to be. For me she's trying to be."

There was something wrong with how he was speaking. I didn't know what had happened to make him this way, but I needed to find a way out of here. For both of us. Only we were chained, and I didn't know if anyone would find me in time.

That cold thought slid up my spine, but I ignored it for now.

"The Montgomerys took care of me, you know."

I looked back at Wyatt when he started talking again.

I tried not to throw up, my whole body shivering, and Wyatt sighed.

"But they're not taking care of you now. And it's okay. I'll do it. The Montgomerys have cared for me, so I'll do the same for you." Wyatt slid a blanket over me, and I wanted to push him away, but I couldn't get free. I was chained to the damn wall.

Wyatt must have seen me jostle the chains, and he sighed.

"Do you know how long it took me to find out how to put in a chain like this by looking on the internet? The internet has a lot of things, but most of the time it's not really helpful. But I found this chat room that really understood. It was like going back in time, you know? With aliases and all that. It was cool. They helped me find the place for the best chains and how to keep you guys safe. And I will keep you safe. I'm not going to hurt you. Not the way you're thinking," he continued quickly. "I would never take what's not mine. But I will make sure that you're taken care of. The world's hard out there, and I'm not going to let the world hurt you."

There was no relief at his statement, only this twisted logic that made me want to curl back and try to get away from his touch. But he slid his hand over my cheek and smiled that innocent smile that told me that there was something really wrong with him.

And none of us had seen it.

"Cora didn't understand. Not until the end. But you will."

He pulled away and began to pace.

"I'm going to have to take you guys away, I think. I shouldn't have taken you from the café. But everyone was gone, and I thought it would be safe. Sebastian doesn't want you anymore, so he's not going to be looking for you. But those other Montgomerys? Those I had to be careful of. They never really watched me, I don't think. But my friends from the internet said I had to be careful. So I'm going to take you guys to another place. A place that they said would be safe to keep you. Just so you guys are safe. Don't worry. I'll keep you safe."

He closed the door, leaving me in the basement, alone with Cora.

I pulled at my chains and I screamed and screamed.

But nobody answered.

Sebastian had to come. He *would* come for me. Or Noah, or someone else. Greer would find me. It might not be until the morning, before they realized that something was wrong at the café and I wasn't there. But they would find me.

I had to have hope.

They would miss me.

And I wouldn't be alone.

I couldn't be alone.

I DIDN'T KNOW HOW LONG I SAT THERE, MY ARM'S aching, but maybe an hour later, Cora woke up, and looked at me with wide eyes and fear etched on her face.

"I'm sorry. I didn't know."

"None of us did. Are you okay?"

Cora gave a soft laugh that had no humor but nodded. "He hasn't touched me in that way. I thought he would. I didn't realize that he was like this. How did I miss it?"

Tears threatened but I shook them off. My heart ached for Cora, but we had to get free somehow. "We all did, don't worry about it. We're going to get out of here. They're going to come for me."

"I've been here for...I don't even know how long. And no one's come for me."

I paused, trying to come to terms with that. "It's still Thursday, I think. It hasn't been that long."

Cora let out a breath, closing her eyes for a moment. "So it's been four days for me, which makes sense. I work from home. And my family calls on Saturdays usually. If I don't talk to them for a couple of days, it's fine. So maybe tomorrow they'll notice that I'm gone, and no one's heard from me." Cora let out a soft laugh. "Isn't that great? No one notices that I'm missing. You didn't."

I winced, my wrists aching right along with my heart. "He said you two broke up. And I didn't have a way to contact you. I'm so sorry."

"I left him. I thought he couldn't love me. And there wasn't a spark. Turns out there was a spark of a different kind. I'm sorry. Maybe I did something?"

"It wasn't you. I promise it wasn't you."

"Okay. I hope so. I just want to go home."

She started crying then, and I tried to reach out to comfort her, but we were chained far enough apart that I couldn't reach her.

I didn't know how we could get out. Maybe when he let us go upstairs to take a bath or something I could find a way. But even that made me want to shudder.

Suddenly there were shouts and screams and loud sounds that made me want to hide.

Cora met my gaze, and then the door slammed open. She screamed and I tried to curl into myself, but this wasn't—

"Ms. Monroe? We've got you, you're safe." The man in front of me looked to the right, cursed, and spoke into the mic on his chest. "We've got another one."

Everything moved quickly after that.

They'd come for me. They'd known I was here.

They knew I was here.

In almost no time, we were out in front of the house, ambulance lights blinding me, making it hard for me to think.

"Let me through. She's my family. Let me through."

At the sound of Sebastian's voice, I looked up and nearly burst into tears.

Noah and Ford were talking to the authorities. I didn't know what was said, but it didn't matter, because then Sebastian was there and touching my face.

"Oh my God, baby. Your beautiful face. Are you okay?"

"I'm okay. Just bruised. And I sort of cut my forehead."

"We need to get you to the hospital, ma'am," the paramedic said, and I nodded.

"Can I come with her?" Sebastian asked,

"It's up to her."

I had so many things to say. It didn't feel real and yet I knew I needed to answer. "Um. Yes, please. I don't know. Just come." I couldn't really focus, because none of this made sense.

But then Sebastian was in the ambulance with me, and we were going to get me checked out. Sebastian didn't say anything on the ride over, just held my hand, and I tried to understand how he was there, how this had all happened.

I just wanted to go home, but we needed to make sure I didn't have a concussion. Four stitches on my forehead, and no concussion later, I sat on the hospital bed, just staring at my hands.

"Did the cops leave?" Noah asked as he came through the doorway, looking between me and Sebastian.

Sebastian hadn't said a word since he got in the ambulance, and I hadn't spoken to him either. I wasn't sure what to say. What I was supposed to say. The authorities had been in and out of the room getting my statement. There were so many unanswered questions, and I knew it could have been a whole lot worse. I suppressed a shudder. So much worse.

Sebastian nodded and Noah stared between us.

"No concussion?"

"No. Just a couple stitches. I can probably go home tonight. The cops are done for now. I still don't really know what's going on."

Noah looked at me, and then at Sebastian. Again.

Noah growled. "Wyatt's locked up. Cora's going to be fine. At least that's what she's saying. My team's with her now. Though it's a little too late, isn't it?"

There was something in his voice, something that worried me.

"It's not your fucking fault," Sebastian growled.

I nodded in agreement. "It's not."

Noah didn't look like he believed us. If anything, his jaw tightened even more. "Wyatt didn't throw any red flags. No one caught it. But he got you and Cora, and we missed it. We didn't even notice that she wasn't around anymore."

"She broke up with him. Everyone missed it. It's not your fault." My mind was going a million different directions and I needed to speak with Sebastian. But Noah needed to be okay too.

"I'm head of security. I do the cyber checks. And I didn't see a thing. So yeah. Let me just figure it the fuck out. But I'm glad you're okay." He looked pointedly at Sebastian. "And I'm glad you're here, too. *Talking.*"

He turned on his heels, leaving us alone.

"I'm sorry," Sebastian said, but I could only see his back.

I wanted to see his face, to figure out what was going on. I'd never felt so lost. "Why are you sorry? It wasn't your fault."

"I'm sorry for hurting you." He turned to me then, his eyes wet.

I held out my hand. "Can you just hold me? I just really need to be held right now."

I watched as his throat worked, and then he sat next to me, his arms around me as I leaned into him.

"It's so stupid. I love you so much, Sebastian. And I

loved you before all this happened. I should have said so. All I could think about when I was down there was that I wasn't going to be able to tell you. That I wasn't going to be able to see your face or Nora's and I'm just so sorry."

He kissed the top of my head. His whole body was shaking. But I was shaking right along with him.

"I was coming over to say I was an idiot. That I love you. And you were gone and I couldn't find you. If the guys didn't have surveillance like they did? I don't know how we would've found you. And it was one of the scariest times of my life."

"I'm sorry I left without trying to fix it. I'm not any good at this."

We pulled apart so we could look at each other, and Sebastian cursed under his breath. "I told you that I didn't know how to date. I didn't know how to be in a relationship. You're my first one as a full-fledged adult, and I'm not handling it very well. I used Nora as an excuse to push you away because I was so damn scared of losing you. And then the world tried to take you away anyway."

I licked my lips and looked down at our clasped hands. "I was so afraid of not being good enough, of trying to take Marley's place, that I walked away. I probably hurt Nora no matter what."

I pressed my lips together and started to cry, but Sebastian wiped my tears away.

"Nora doesn't know what happened. She just thinks

you're working a lot. She's with my parents right now. I don't know how to tell her any of this. Don't know if I should. I'm also not sure if I should keep secrets from my kid. This parenting thing is hard. It's been hard doing it alone, but it was nice having you around, because I love you, and I love the way that you are with her. I don't know what's going to happen next. But I also know that I almost lost you because some damn idiot thought he could protect you better than I could."

"Please don't compare yourself to Wyatt. There is something actually wrong with him."

"Are you okay for real?"

I rubbed at my wrists, the bruises had started to pop up. "I'll be okay. It's just so weird. I think I'm still on an adrenaline high. I don't want to fight like this with you anymore. I don't want to feel like I'm not good enough."

"That was never the case. I promise you. You are not Marley. But I don't mean that in a bad way."

I laughed. "I get you."

"Do you? Because I want to make sure you do. I'm trying to figure out this whole relationship and being a dad thing. But I want to figure it out with you. The Sebastian that is here right now, the Sebastian in front of you, he loves you. I'm not that man from our past. And we can't go back and wonder what-ifs and how to fix things. I learned that the hard way. So I want to go forward, look into the future, and to know that we're going to do it together. I don't know what that means exactly. But I know I want to take our time and figure it out. I want to be open and honest with my daughter. Because she loves you too. And that means that however we make this work, we're a family. In the complicated way that we Montgomerys do it."

I was openly crying now, holding him tight.

"Tonight was so scary. But I'm okay. And I would love to figure our future out together. Because I love that little girl too."

"Good. Because I'm pretty sure she's not letting you go." He paused. "And neither am I."

Then his lips were on mine, and I could barely hold back my tears.

The door opened again and the nurse came in to see why my heart rate was skyrocketing. She shook her head, and let the other Montgomerys in. Of course, because they were my family too. My parents followed them, having driven the hour to get here. And I knew that this was my future. What I had never allowed myself to believe could ever happen.

I pressed my hand to my neck, and my eyes widened. "My necklace. Where did my necklace go?"

"Everything you were wearing went with the authorities, but we'll get it back for you. I promise," Aria said from my side, where she held tight to my other hand.

"Thank you. Thank all you all for being here."

My parents came forward and Sebastian moved away so they could hug me and then I was holding back tears as everyone took turns coming in the room so we didn't annoy the nursing staff by overcrowding the room.

Ford was the last one to leave—other than Sebastian —and he stared at me.

"What is it, Ford?" I asked, my voice hoarse. I leaned into Sebastian as he held me like he never wanted to let me go.

"We're sorry, you know. That we didn't know about Wyatt. I never want you to feel that you're unsafe at your place, so if you want, we can go over security again and make sure you feel safe there."

My heart swelled and I smiled up at him, tired and feeling like I was having an out of body experience. "Your cameras figured out who took me and you were able to give that to the police so they could go to Wyatt's house and find him. It worked."

"You were still taken," Sebastian growled, and Ford looked like he'd been kicked.

"Because a man I trusted walked into my unlocked place of business when I was alone. I'm usually never alone. And if I hadn't had the door locked between the places, someone would have heard the commotion, like when I screamed when Noah startled me."

Ford shook his head. "No. You don't get to blame yourself for Wyatt's actions. We're going to take what happened here and learn from it. Our family is going to be safe." He spoke as if he were a Montgomery, though I knew he was a Cage and had a large family of his own. But then again, the Montgomerys had a way of bringing people closer together.

"We'll make sure we're always safe. I'm never letting you and Nora out of my sight again."

From the growl in Sebastian's voice, I had a feeling I wasn't going to change his mind. At least not tonight.

"Okay. I trust you. This is on Wyatt, though. Don't let Noah blame himself either. We all thought we could trust Wyatt."

From the dark look that crossed Ford's eyes, I had a feeling he didn't think Noah was going to let himself off from this. But there was nothing I could do about that right then.

Eventually, Sebastian and I were left alone. After a sweet phone call to Nora where we promised to see her soon, I cuddled into the man I loved and sighed.

"It's going to take me a long time to get the image of you in that ambulance out of my mind."

I knew the image of Marley in the hospital was also in his mind, as it was in mine, even though I hadn't been there. But there was nothing I could do but hold him and never let go.

"Same here. But we're together and going to be okay. I don't think I can handle anything else."

He kissed the top of my head and I closed my eyes, oddly content, even though I knew sleep wouldn't come easy.

"We're together. So yeah, we can handle this. Because I've got you. I love you, Raven."

The words slid through me and I smiled. "I love you, too, Seb."

I couldn't help but wonder exactly how I'd come to be here. He wasn't what I ever thought I would have. But he was everything I needed and now I just wanted to go home and start our life.

Chapter 21

Sebastian

"WE'RE GOING TO BE LATE IF WE DON'T HURRY."

I smiled down at Raven, moving her hair from her face as the water rained down on us. "We're going to also have to be very quiet, because Nora is bouncing around the living room, waiting for us to get you ready."

"I think I can be quiet," she whispered, and then her hand was on my dick, and it was hard for me to think.

I crushed my mouth to hers, water sliding over us. I parted her folds, my fingers sliding over her clit. When she shivered, I grinned against her, playing with her before I inserted one finger and then another. She groaned, spreading her legs for me, and I continued to pump in and out of her, matching the rhythm she was pumping on my dick, using the soap so it was a smooth glide.

I humped against her, thrusting into her hand, and before I knew it, she came on my hand, a quick motion that had her shaking, and I gripped her hip, keeping her steady.

"You okay? Don't want you sliding in here."

"Then you better get inside me and keep me steady. I'm really glad that your shower has a bench."

I grinned, then adjusted us so I could slide deep inside her in one thrust.

We didn't need a condom, not now. We were tested, exclusive, and she was mine.

I licked at her neck, played with her breasts, loving the way she tugged on my nipple rings.

When she came again, I followed, filling her as I continued to pump my hips, my knees shaking.

"We're going to use all the hot water," she whispered against me, kissing my throat.

I pinched her hip, and then slid out of her, grateful we had already washed our hair.

We were quick cleaning up after that, and then we tumbled out of the shower, laughing.

We got ready quickly, getting dressed first so Nora could run in, talking about how excited she was for the recital that night.

"Are you going to wear your blue dress?" Nora asked, bouncing on her feet.

Raven and I didn't live together, not yet, but she spent the night at my place more often than not. Nora even had a little bed over at Raven's place, for the few nights that we spent over there.

In the weeks since everything happened, since I'd almost lost her, we had gone full into who we were. Into the relationship we wanted.

Nora only knew parts of what had happened, she didn't need to know it all, at least not yet. But she knew Raven had been hurt. She was an adorable little nurse to bring Raven back to full health. And during that time Raven had stayed with us, and we had fallen full swing into the family that we were becoming.

Every time I saw them together, it reminded me that Marley was still here with us, just in a different sense. She had brought Nora into my life, and I would be forever grateful for that.

And now I loved Raven. And the thing was, a human was able to love more than one person. They were able to open up their heart as full as they needed to. Marley was my past, Raven and Nora were my future.

I was one blessed man, even if it took me nearly losing everything to realize that.

Raven met my gaze at Nora's question, and then nodded down at my daughter.

"I was going to. I think it will match your dress perfectly, don't you think?"

"I think it's perfect. And I'm excited to go over to Grandma and Grandpa's for dinner after!" She paused. "Daddy's mom and dad. Not other Grandpa and Grandma. Although I'm going over there tomorrow. And I'm really excited because we're going to make cookies!"

The idea that my daughter was excited to go to Marley's parents was still a surprise, but ever since our talk—our blowout—things had changed. I knew they were going to therapy now, something they should have done five years ago, like I had, but there was no way to force someone into healing. But things were better for now. They weren't perfect, and they would never be, but we were finding a way to work together. The fact that they no longer talked down to me or made my daughter cry meant something.

"I have to blow dry my hair real quick, and then I'll be ready to go."

"Can I help?" Nora asked, and Raven smiled and nodded. "You've got it."

I'm pretty sure it took twice as long as it would have without Nora's help.

They looked adorable though, and I loved watching the two get ready.

Nora had plenty of women in her life. My sisters, my mother, and all of my cousins and aunts. But she never had a mother. And one day, when I proposed—and it would be soon, even though it seemed like it was just yesterday that I fell in love with her—we would be a new family figuring out who we were. This wasn't the family I thought I'd have, but it was the family I had now, the family that was exactly what I wanted.

I was damn blessed to have these women in my life, the girls that were my everything.

I was so grateful that Nora loved Raven, and she didn't feel the lack of not having Marley. If anything, she had the future she wanted.

"Do you have your costume?" I asked.

Nora turned to me, wide-eyed. "I do."

"Why don't you double check, and we'll make sure Raven's all ready to go. We need to meet up with Molly and Shane and their families for photos."

"Okay!"

I moved out of the way as Nora barreled past, going a thousand miles per hour, like always.

"She's too cute, but I have no idea how you did this alone for so long."

"I was never alone. I had the Montgomerys. And now I have you. So maybe I will actually be able to sleep in once in a while."

"Sure. Like you know how to sleep in." She rolled her eyes before moving to slide her feet into her heels. She was so damn beautiful. Sometimes it was hard to breathe just looking at her.

"I love you."

"I'm never going to tire of hearing that. I love you too." She kissed me softly, and then we were out the door, star costume in hand for the winter recital.

The children were shouting and full of sugar and exhaustedly happy as they did their evening recital for the dance studio. They already had the school recital for the winter break, and the soccer season was over for now.

There should've been a break for us just to breathe, but of course that wasn't the case.

"So, after this we have dinner with your family, and then all of the holiday chaos with presents and pictures and food and family. And then school and work and sports start right back up?" Raven asked, laughing.

"Pretty much. It's a little exhausting. But we'll figure it out."

She smiled at me and I hugged her, as we watched Nora dance along as a star.

My immediate family were in the audience, as we hadn't wanted to take over the entire auditorium.

After this, we would all head over to my parents' house and have dinner. We'd eat too much cheese, laugh too hard, and have fun.

I was so damn happy that somehow we had made this work. Somehow we had found a way to not break when the world had come against us.

I kissed the top of Raven's head as I watched Nora dance along the stage.

She was a star in every way possible, and she was mine. And one day soon, she would be ours.

I thought about the ring I had already picked out, the one I would use to ask Raven to be my wife.

I had an idea in mind, one that involved Nora, if she wanted.

We had gone full steam ahead, and now we were finding our place. But I knew I was holding my future wife and watching our daughter on the stage. This had been a long time coming, but this was everything.

And as Raven smiled up at me, I grinned right back, and I couldn't wait for that evening, and then the next morning, and the next everything.

After all, this was just the beginning.

Chapter 22

Greer

I wasn't lonely per se. I couldn't be lonely when I was surrounded by so many people. My boss, my co-owners, and Raven's new family had practically adopted me. I hadn't expected that. But I was happy.

I loved my job. I loved coffee. I was addicted to coffee. But thankfully my job kept me surrounded by those beans, so it was perfect.

I had my best friend, who included me in everything even as she connected with her past and found her future. I wasn't being left behind, and I was grateful. Because I was happy.

So I couldn't be lonely.

Okay, maybe I was lonely in the sense that I couldn't remember the last time I had sex, but that was beside the point. I had a vibrator. I had my hand. I knew how to get myself off better than anyone.

And all I could do was think about a certain face. No, that was a lie. There were two faces.

Two faces that haunted my wet dreams.

I knew there were poly relationships out there, in fact there were even a few in the Montgomerys. So I knew that they could be healthy, that they weren't doomed to jealousy and pain.

But that wasn't for me. It couldn't be for me. I wasn't that lucky.

I shook my head as I made another latte and worked on foam art, though I couldn't help but look at the front door that they could walk through at any moment as they were wont to do.

No, they weren't for me.

I sighed. "Not for me," I mumbled.

"What is that?" Raven asked.

I shook my head. "Just mumbling to myself. I think I need more coffee."

"I really don't think you need more coffee," Raven teased.

I rolled my eyes, but she might be right. I might have a little too much coffee in me. But it was fine. It was the only thing I had in my life that I could count on.

No, that was a complete lie. Because I had Raven. But she had her whole new life. Her new family. And I didn't want to stand in the way. I was really good at standing in the way.

It was what I had been taught most of my life—that I was always in the way.

I looked up as they walked past. It was them. It was always *them*. I needed to stop. It wasn't smart to think about them. It wasn't smart to watch them.

And yet I couldn't help it.

Only they weren't for me. Hell, I didn't even know if they were for each other.

Because when they looked at each other, I saw that intense heat, though I didn't think they did. I saw the friendship that was always there. Or maybe I was just seeing things because I was attracted to both of them.

But Noah and Ford walked past our window and didn't stop in. I held back my disappointment. I didn't need to see them every day. I didn't need to speak with them. I didn't need to guess their orders.

I had a bit of a crush. That was it. I was tempted. But I wasn't going to succumb. I couldn't. Not when they had each other.

I was not going to have Noah or Ford. It would just be a mess. A complete mess. So I would be their friend.

That friend.

I made another cup of coffee, I smiled at Raven, and I ignored the tempting men on the other side of the building. The ones that haunted my dreams and made me want too much. I didn't need them. No, I needed somebody else. So I would find a date, one that had nothing to do with the Montgomerys, or their best friends.

Chapter 23

Noah

I SLOWLY LICKED MY WAY UP HIS BACK, BITING DOWN ON the strong cord of muscle where his neck and his shoulder met, my hands digging into his hips.

"More," he whispered.

I groaned, biting harder, before I licked the hurt, just a little mark that would remind him I had been there. I kissed down his shoulders, down his back, before squeezing his ass, and pressing myself against him.

"If you don't fuck me soon, I'm going to turn you over and take my turn."

I grinned, my head a little dizzy, the drinks having been a little too strong.

But it was the only way I could get this brave, then I'd be able to blame it on the alcohol later.

I turned to the man in my arms, crushing my mouth to his. He tasted of booze and mint and promise.

Of broken promises, of mistakes.

He reached between us, gripping my dick, and I groaned, pumping into his fist.

"Fine, I'll just take matters into my own hands."

He went to his knees, and before I could do anything, he had his mouth around my dick, and I was thrusting into him.

I gripped his hair, forcing my cock into his mouth, down his throat. He gagged, but kept going. He squeezed my hips, then my ass, spreading me as he continued to bob his head, taking me hard, not backing down.

I pulled away as my balls drew tight, because I didn't want to come right now.

No, I wanted to be inside him.

I pulled him to his feet, pressing our dicks together. When he gripped us both, the friction nearly sending me over the edge, I shuddered.

I pushed him down on the bed and grabbed the lube.

"Fine," I growled.

I was going to remember this, and that meant I wasn't drunk enough.

He seemed to understand what I was thinking, and a wave of hurt crashed over his face before he pushed it away and spread himself for me. I readied him, then myself, then I faced him, before I slowly slid balls deep inside him. He was tight, damn tight, but it didn't matter, I just needed him, needed to fuck him. Needed to forget.

He pushed back on me, legs around my waist as we moved, fucking each other with abandon, as if nothing mattered, as if everything mattered.

I pulled out and he went to all fours. I slammed back in, riding him into oblivion. I slid my hand around, gripping his cock. I pumped him as I fucked him from behind. He groaned my name, and then he was warm over my hand as he came, and I filled him, both of us shaking.

This wasn't our first time, but it had to be our last.

It always had to be our last.

"Well. That happened," Ford whispered, as I slowly pulled out of him, reaching for the towel to clean us up.

I didn't look at him, I couldn't. All I could do was hang my head in shame and hate myself once again.

Because I was using him. We used each other.

And I hated myself.

"Shit," Ford whispered, as he sat next to me, hands on his knees.

"Shit."

"So, I guess we're just going to continue to fuck each other and not talk about it?" my best friend asked.

"It can't happen again." I had said those words before, but this time I meant them. Even through the booze haze, it couldn't happen again.

"We live together. We work together. And you're my best friend, Noah. Why can't it happen again?"

"We can't do this. If we do? We break everything you just said."

"I know," Ford said. And that was the problem, he did. He knew we couldn't, just like I did. And yet here we were, fucking each other because I was so damn weak.

"We can't let it happen again."

Ford didn't say anything for so long, I wasn't sure what he was thinking. And that was the problem, I usually knew what Ford was thinking. Finally, he stood up, naked and gorgeous. Long lines of muscles, tattoos, a few scars. He had been through hell before, had come out stronger for it.

And I had always wanted him. And maybe that was our problem.

"You're directing your anger over what happened on me. I get it. You hate that you missed it. Only you didn't. We didn't. You don't get to fuck me because you're angry. Fuck me because you want to."

At that, Ford Cage, my best friend, the lover that I knew I could never have, left, and I hung my head down, shame crawling over me.

I hated myself.

But it was the one thing I seemed to be good at these days.

Untitled

BONUS EPILOGUE

Sebastian

"Why am I suddenly nervous?" Raven stood by the table, wringing her hands in front of her. When she bit her teeth into her bottom lip, my cock noticed, and I had to swallow hard.

That woman just did things to me, I couldn't help it.

I moved forward and brushed my fingers along her cheekbone.

"We don't have to do this today. We can do this any day, or no day at all." I grinned, looked down at myself and then back up at her. "I'm pretty sure I have enough ink for the both of us."

She smiled at me, before rolling her eyes. "I think you have enough ink for the whole family."

"I'm not so sure about that," Leif put in from his station. "My dad has even more than he does."

"He's had a few more years to work on it," I added, a little aggrieved.

"It's okay you know. You don't have to be the best at this."

I growled at her.

"As I'm going to be the only one who ever touches this skin, I better be the fucking best at it."

"Daddy said a curse word," my little girl giggled beside me, as she danced.

I cursed under my breath, hoping that she didn't notice. My brother laughed at me from where he stood with Nora.

"You are really bad at this," Gus said.

"I'm horrible at this," I said. "Even with all this practice. You'd think over five years that I'd be good. But I think my cursing just gets worse."

"It's okay, Daddy. I know not to curse. Because it's for adults."

"It is," Raven said sagely, her eyes twinkling.

"And when Shane cursed because his daddy did, his mom got so mad."

Raven and I both choked back our laughter.

"Like we said, we can say the words because we're

adults, and we're trying not to use them around you, but sometimes they just come right out."

"It's okay. I don't mind. But when I'm an adult, I'm going to curse all the time. Because it looks like fun."

"You really only have yourself to blame here," Leif mumbled under his breath.

"I have heard both of your sons say bad words," I said, staring at him.

"All because of you."

"You might want to blame Brooke for that one."

"I heard that," Leif's wife said from the back office where she and Lake were going over a few things.

"Now really, tell me when you're getting started on Raven. I want to see."

"I want to see too," Nora said as she clapped her hands.

"You see? She wants to see too."

"Okay, I can do this. Just tell me what you need."

I raised a brow and she just grinned. "Not that," she said.

"What is she talking about? Does she need kisses? You should give her kisses."

Raven blushed, and I held back a laugh.

"We can do kisses. We all like kisses."

I reached down and began to tickle my daughter, who giggled, and then Raven joined in, and it felt like we were a family.

A new kind of family. One that was just for us.

We would never forget Marley. We couldn't. She was part of us, and I could see her in my little girl's eyes.

But we could move on into the future while acknowledging our past. It had taken me a long time to get to this point.

"Okay. I'm ready."

I nodded, and then brought up the stencil.

We had decided on an outline of a dove, flying into clouds. Doves were always Raven's favorite bird, other than her namesake. Of course.

So on the other side of the dove, a raven would be waiting, in a kaleidoscope of light and shading.

We both knew who the dove represented.

Marley was etched on my skin as well, why shouldn't she be on Raven's?

I had been worried at first, thinking that would bring too many bad memories for Raven. But she had wanted it. And I was going to be the one to do it. I worked with the stencil, placing it exactly where we wanted it to go on her shoulder, and when we were ready, we began.

Nora watched, fascinated. This wasn't her first time watching me do a tattoo, but it was the first time where it felt like we were a whole new family, figuring things out.

It was exciting, worrying, but it was our future. I could not believe that this was my life now. I wouldn't have thought it possible even six months ago. But here I was, tattooing the woman that I loved, the woman that would be my wife, and would help raise our daughter.

Our daughter. We weren't going to replace Marley, we could never, but we were going to be a family. And that was something I never thought possible.

I finished the tattoo, as it was mostly an outline, with some shading. But we wanted it to be simple for her first tattoo, and it was damn good if I said so myself. Raven was the perfect client, and I loved being able to touch her skin. It always made me sound like Buffalo Bill when I said that, a character from a movie far older than I was. But the inside jokes about it with our family meant I had of course seen the movie multiple times.

When I pulled away, Nora clapped, dancing around, and Gus took a video of her, just laughing.

"You do good work, brother."

"Let me see," Raven said. I held up a mirror, and she gasped. "It's beautiful."

Tears began to slide down her cheeks and I kissed them away, brushing her hair from her face.

"You're the beautiful one. You are a perfect canvas."

"Well, that's a good line," Nick muttered, and I flipped him off, wincing when Nora laughed.

"You're getting worse in your old age," Gus teased, and I barely resisted the urge to flip him off, before I leaned down, and pressed my lips to Raven's.

"I love you. Thank you for letting me be your first."

She blushed again, before she leaned down and took Nora's hand.

"So you like it?"

"I love it. It's the best. Of course it's the best though. Because Daddy's the best."

I beamed, my chest filling. I couldn't help it. She was a daddy's girl, and I was damn proud.

I leaned down and picked Nora up. When she wrapped her arms around my shoulders, she kissed my cheek, so I kissed her forehead.

I stood with my girls, in the place that I had built with my family, our future, our legacy.

And I knew that this was exactly what I had needed, what I had wanted, even if I hadn't realized.

I was ready for the next step. For Raven to be my wife, for our family to grow, and for our paths to merge.

It had been a long time coming, but I wouldn't have it any other way.

NEXT IN THE MONTGOMERY INK LEGACY SERIES:
The next Montgomery triad is here with Best Friend Temptation.

A Note from Carrie Ann Ryan

Thank you so much for reading **LONGTIME CRUSH!**

Oh boy. I knew this story would be hard the moment I met Sebastian. But I didn't realize Raven would be the one to soothe that ache. Though in reality, I should have.

I loved writing this romance and this story. Nora is now one of my favorite characters ever and I knew writing a slight time jump would bring me her joy.

I hope you loved this romance as much as I did!

Coming up next? Noah, Ford, and Greer make up a triad that is going to just but…ugh…I am not ready. But I hope you are!

The Montgomery Ink Legacy Series:
Book 1: Bittersweet Promises
Book 2: At First Meet

NEXT IN THE MONTGOMERY INK LEGACY SERIES:
Noah, Ford, and Greer change everything in Best Friend Temptation.

If you want to make sure you know what's coming next from me, you can sign up for my newsletter at www. CarrieAnnRyan.com; follow me on twitter at @CarrieAnnRyan, or like my Facebook page. I also have a Facebook Fan Club where we have trivia, chats, and other goodies. You guys are the reason I get to do what I do and I thank you.

Make sure you're signed up for my MAILING LIST so you can know when the next releases are available as well as find giveaways and FREE READS.

Happy Reading!

Also from Carrie Ann Ryan

The Montgomery Ink Legacy Series:
Book 1: Bittersweet Promises
Book 2: At First Meet
Book 2.5: Happily Ever Never
Book 3: Longtime Crush
Book 4: Best Friend Temptation
Book 5: Last First Kiss

The Wilder Brothers Series:
Book 1: One Way Back to Me
Book 2: Always the One for Me
Book 3: The Path to You
Book 4: Coming Home for Us
Book 5: Stay Here With Me
Book 6: Finding the Road to Us
Book 7: A Wilder Wedding

Also from Carrie Ann Ryan

The First Time Series:
Book 1: Good Time Boyfriend

The Aspen Pack Series:
Book 1: Etched in Honor
Book 2: Hunted in Darkness
Book 3: Mated in Chaos
Book 4: Harbored in Silence
Book 5: Marked in Flames

The Montgomery Ink: Fort Collins Series:
Book 1: Inked Persuasion
Book 2: Inked Obsession
Book 3: Inked Devotion
Book 3.5: Nothing But Ink
Book 4: Inked Craving
Book 5: Inked Temptation

The Montgomery Ink: Boulder Series:
Book 1: Wrapped in Ink
Book 2: Sated in Ink
Book 3: Embraced in Ink
Book 3: Moments in Ink
Book 4: Seduced in Ink
Book 4.5: Captured in Ink
Book 4.7: Inked Fantasy
Book 4.8: A Very Montgomery Christmas

Montgomery Ink: Colorado Springs

Book 1: Fallen Ink

Book 2: Restless Ink

Book 2.5: Ashes to Ink

Book 3: Jagged Ink

Book 3.5: Ink by Numbers

Montgomery Ink Denver:

Book 0.5: Ink Inspired

Book 0.6: Ink Reunited

Book 1: Delicate Ink

Book 1.5: Forever Ink

Book 2: Tempting Boundaries

Book 3: Harder than Words

Book 3.5: Finally Found You

Book 4: Written in Ink

Book 4.5: Hidden Ink

Book 5: Ink Enduring

Book 6: Ink Exposed

Book 6.5: Adoring Ink

Book 6.6: Love, Honor, & Ink

Book 7: Inked Expressions

Book 7.3: Dropout

Book 7.5: Executive Ink

Book 8: Inked Memories

Book 8.5: Inked Nights

Book 8.7: Second Chance Ink

Book 8.5: Montgomery Midnight Kisses

Bonus: Inked Kingdom

The On My Own Series:

Book 0.5: My First Glance

Book 1: My One Night

Book 2: My Rebound

Book 3: My Next Play

Book 4: My Bad Decisions

The Promise Me Series:

Book 1: Forever Only Once

Book 2: From That Moment

Book 3: Far From Destined

Book 4: From Our First

The Less Than Series:

Book 1: Breathless With Her

Book 2: Reckless With You

Book 3: Shameless With Him

The Fractured Connections Series:

Book 1: Breaking Without You

Book 2: Shouldn't Have You

Book 3: Falling With You

Book 4: Taken With You

The Whiskey and Lies Series:

Book 1: Whiskey Secrets

Book 2: <u>Whiskey Reveals</u>
Book 3: <u>Whiskey Undone</u>

The Gallagher Brothers Series:
Book 1: <u>Love Restored</u>
Book 2: <u>Passion Restored</u>
Book 3: <u>Hope Restored</u>

The Ravenwood Coven Series:
Book 1: Dawn Unearthed
Book 2: Dusk Unveiled
Book 3: Evernight Unleashed

The Talon Pack:
Book 1: <u>Tattered Loyalties</u>
Book 2: <u>An Alpha's Choice</u>
Book 3: <u>Mated in Mist</u>
Book 4: <u>Wolf Betrayed</u>
Book 5: <u>Fractured Silence</u>
Book 6: <u>Destiny Disgraced</u>
Book 7: <u>Eternal Mourning</u>
Book 8: <u>Strength Enduring</u>
Book 9: <u>Forever Broken</u>
Book 10: Mated in Darkness
Book 11: Fated in Winter

Redwood Pack Series:
Book 1: <u>An Alpha's Path</u>

Book 2: <u>A Taste for a Mate</u>

Book 3: <u>Trinity Bound</u>

Book 3.5: <u>A Night Away</u>

Book 4: <u>Enforcer's Redemption</u>

Book 4.5: <u>Blurred Expectations</u>

Book 4.7: <u>Forgiveness</u>

Book 5: <u>Shattered Emotions</u>

Book 6: <u>Hidden Destiny</u>

Book 6.5: <u>A Beta's Haven</u>

Book 7: <u>Fighting Fate</u>

Book 7.5: <u>Loving the Omega</u>

Book 7.7: <u>The Hunted Heart</u>

Book 8: <u>Wicked Wolf</u>

The Elements of Five Series:

Book 1: From Breath and Ruin

Book 2: From Flame and Ash

Book 3: From Spirit and Binding

Book 4: From Shadow and Silence

Dante's Circle Series:

Book 1: <u>Dust of My Wings</u>

Book 2: <u>Her Warriors' Three Wishes</u>

Book 3: <u>An Unlucky Moon</u>

Book 3.5: <u>His Choice</u>

Book 4: <u>Tangled Innocence</u>

Book 5: <u>Fierce Enchantment</u>

Book 6: <u>An Immortal's Song</u>

Book 7: <u>Prowled Darkness</u>
Book 8: Dante's Circle Reborn

Holiday, Montana Series:
Book 1: <u>Charmed Spirits</u>
Book 2: <u>Santa's Executive</u>
Book 3: <u>Finding Abigail</u>
Book 4: <u>Her Lucky Love</u>
Book 5: Dreams of Ivory

The Branded Pack Series:
(Written with Alexandra Ivy)
Book 1: <u>Stolen and Forgiven</u>
Book 2: <u>Abandoned and Unseen</u>
Book 3: <u>Buried and Shadowed</u>

About the Author

Carrie Ann Ryan is the New York Times and USA Today bestselling author of contemporary, paranormal, and young adult romance. Her works include the Montgomery Ink, Redwood Pack, Fractured Connections, and Elements of Five series, which have sold over 3.0 million books worldwide. She started writing while in graduate school for her advanced degree in chemistry and hasn't stopped since. Carrie Ann has written over seventy-five novels and novellas with more in the works. When she's not losing herself in her emotional and action-packed worlds, she's reading as much as she can while wrangling her clowder of cats who have more followers than she does.

www.CarrieAnnRyan.com